MAIA DYLAN

EVERNIGHT PUBLISHING ®

www.evernightpublishing.com

JUSTICE FOR VIOLET

Copyright© 2017

Maia Dylan

Editor: Karyn White

Cover Artist: Jay Aheer

ISBN: 978-1-77339-368-1

MAIA DYLAN

DEDICATION

For my best friend who is the hardest working mother of two I have ever met. You continue to amaze me with your never ending capacity for love and just how damn calm you are when your kids spill nail polish on the carpet. Can't wait for our next girls' night out! Margaritas on me.

And to my hubby, who puts up with my girls' nights out and the fallout that may come from them.

MAIA DYLAN

JUSTICE FOR VIOLET

Retribution, 1

Maia Dylan

Copyright © 2017

Prologue

\<opentransmission\>
DOCUMENTTYPE: Open letter to the people of
Chicago
DISTRIBUTION: All known online and social media
forms
SUBJECT: We are a city at war
SOURCE: IEH
There is a plague in our city, an infestation of evil intent
that is winding itself around the very fabric of the place
we call home, and if we do not take a stand and eradicate
this evil, it will take hold to the point where Chicago as
we know it, will be lost.

We hear it in the news every day, and shake our heads in
sympathy at the lives this infestation takes. We see it in
our streets and turn our heads out of fear for our own
safety, and we tell ourselves it could never happen to us.
But when we turn our backs on what is happening right
in front of us, when we do not stand up to the
intimidation and persecution of Roberto Santiago and
what he allows his men to do in our communities, are we

not just as guilty?

How many more people have to be killed before you summon the courage to stand with those who fight against this plague? And there are those that fight, and their numbers are growing. Santiago must be stopped.

By any means. At any cost.

Chapter One

Jacob Williams used every ounce of speed his shifter ability could give him to get to the front door of Black Ridge House as fast as possible. Seeing as how he was a leopard shifter, he had considerable speed, and made it there before the roar that had broken the night silence from outside had completely died away. His Alpha, Kieran Murphy, was a lion, and his roar of agony had ripped through the house and the forest around them, calling every Black Ridge Pride member in the vicinity to him. Jacob sensed rather than heard the other shifters in the house heading in the same direction. He reached the door first and threw it open.

Kieran knelt on the drive in front of the house beside one of the black jeeps the pride preferred to use when patrolling. Jacob leaped from the porch and fell to his knees beside his Alpha.

"Fuck, Jason!" Jason had only just started patrolling, and he and his brother Vernon had been one of the first young leopards Jacob had trained as Enforcers.

The younger man blinked slowly as his gaze turned from his Alpha to look up at Jacob. "Th-the wounds won't heal, Jacob." Jason's voice was weak, and his body shook, no doubt from shock. He bled sluggishly from two gaping bullet wounds in his upper chest, and Jacob shared a shaken look with his Alpha. "Vernon is dead. I got him in the back. I—I couldn't l-leave him there. How could I tell my mom that I left my younger brother dead on the streets?" Jason's teeth chattered, the cold another indication that Jason had lost a lot of blood. "I couldn't do that."

"Mason!" Jacob yelled out when he saw his brother heading in their direction. "Grab the medical kit!" Mason jolted with shock, but ran to do as he'd asked. It wasn't often a shifter with healing abilities required a medical kit, and when they did it was usually bad. This was no exception.

"It's okay, Jase," Kieran said gently as he kept pressure on the wounds. "You brought him home, and we'll get you fixed up in no time. We'll find the fuckers that left you there and took Vernon from us."

Jason's eyes slid to Kieran. "They didn't leave us, Alpha. Santiago's men ambushed us near the Lincoln Memorial. We were just finishing our patrol and they jumped us. Vernon shifted and attacked, but they shot Vernon, then me. Vernon shifted back. Then they let me leave. The bastards were laughing the whole time."

Jacob frowned. "What do you mean they let you leave?"

Jason lifted up a cell phone Jacob hadn't even realized he'd had in his hands. "They gave me this to give to you, Kieran," Jason said in a voice barely above a whisper. "I don't feel as cold as I did before. Do you think I am starting to heal now, Alpha?"

Kieran inhaled sharply then leaned down, putting his face close to Jason's. "You bet you are. You are one of my strongest, Jason, and no fucking bullet is going to take you from the pride. You'll get better and we'll find the bastards that did this to you."

Jacob watched as the light of life faded in Jason's eyes and his heart bled for the loss not only of a member of the pride, but someone he considered a friend.

Kieran sat completely still for a moment, staring into Jason's face, before reaching out and gently closing his eyes. Jacob felt grief and rage building within him, and he looked around at the faces of the pride who had gathered around them, his gaze falling on his older brother, knowing that the pain and horror he saw on Mason's face must have been mirrored in his own.

The sound of a phone ringing hit the night, and Kieran jerked his arm up. The cell phone Jason had handed him was ringing in his hand. Sliding his bloodstained finger across the screen to answer the call, Kieran lifted the phone to his ear. Shifters had enhanced levels of hearing so every one of the pride heard the voice on the other end of the phone.

"Did the dumb shit die yet?" The smug arrogance in Santiago's tone came through clear. "I do so hope I haven't called while he's going through his final death throes. They can be very entertaining but oh so dramatic, can't they? I'd hate for you to miss them."

"You think you've made a fucking point with this?" Kieran asked in a deadly tone, his voice harsh, and Jacob heard more than a thread of the man's lion in his voice.

"The point!" Santiago yelled. "The point is that now I have something that makes it possible to kill you bastards. These bullets make you take human form, and they inhibit your healing. If we shoot you in a place that would kill a normal human being, then you fucking animals will die, too. You've lost your advantage, Murphy. Now, you have seven days to get the fuck out of Chicago, because if you don't then it will be open season on every single one of you abominations."

Kieran growled low in his chest. "You've killed too many innocents already, you narcissistic son of a bitch. This. Ends. You can shove your ultimatums right up your ass. We don't need your seven days. You want war? Then war is what you will get. I will make you this promise, Santiago—you will die screaming while you watch as my lion eats your heart in front of you. Look for me soon, asshole. I'm. Coming. For you."

Kieran crushed the phone with one hand, effectively ending the call. He inhaled sharply, threw his head back and roared, loud and long into the night. Feeling the emotions and pain within him swelling to epic proportions, Jacob was helpless not to follow his lead, and he, too, threw his head back and roared. His pride had lost two of their own, and the loss was felt throughout the entire pride. Roars and cries of pain echoed around them, and Jacob had to fight the need his leopard had to change, run into the forest, and never look back until he had bled the bastards who had done this. But he couldn't. There was work to do here first before they could avenge their brothers.

But vengeance would be theirs, and Jacob vowed that he would be standing there in the moment his alpha killed Santiago. He planned to be there to utter the last words the man would ever hear, and he would do anything and everything to ensure that happened.

****

"Hey, *chica*, where you going so fast?"

Violet Riccitelli ignored the man's question, gripped her purse tight to her side, hunched her shoulders a little higher and stepped up her pace.

"Oh, come on now, *chica,* don't be like that. We only want to talk with you."

Violet very much doubted that was the case.

She walked swiftly around the corner and knew that the three men who had started following her as soon as she stepped out the subway exit, made the turn just behind her. The air was cool for an October evening, so there weren't as many people walking around as there normally might have been.

Violet saw an alleyway coming up and moved slightly away from the opening, just in case there were more of them, and one was waiting for her in the shadows beyond the darkened entrance. She sped up even further, but as soon as she had stepped clear of the first building, one of the men behind her moved up beside her and pushed her hard through the entrance. Violet cried out as she stumbled into the alleyway.

"Wh-what are you doing?" she asked in a voice that trembled.

"Oh, so now you want to talk to me," the man who had first spoken to her jeered. "You weren't such a talkative little slut a minute ago, now were you?"

Violet stumbled back into the alleyway, looking left and right for a way to escape. "Help me! Someone help me, please!"

The three men laughed and stepped toward her menacingly.

The Hispanic man in the middle sneered at her. "This is Santiago territory. Ain't no one gonna help you, *chica*. It's not that kinda neighborhood."

"This one is pretty," one of the other men said in a voice that sounded like he smoked at least a pack a day. "The last ones have been pretty fucking ugly. I want this one to stay pretty when I fuck her. Then, we'll take a knife to that face so she leaves here an ugly cunt like the others."

The three men kept advancing in her direction, so Violet kept stumbling backward, making wordless sounds of panic. When she passed the last dumpster and was pressed up against the concrete wall at the back of the alley, her only avenue of escape involved getting past the three men in front of her.

"There's nowhere left to hide now, little girl." The third man, who up until that point had remained silent, spoke this time. "We're gonna fuck you up so damn bad, your own momma ain't gonna recognize you."

Violet had been huddling against the back wall of the alley, whimpering in fear, but now suddenly stood tall. "Well, yeah, I kinda thought that was the point of the whole push the innocent girl into the dark alley and threaten her routine you guys have got going on. But when exactly are you going to stop talking about it and actually do something?"

Violet stared at the three men standing opposite her in the alley and not for the first time, wished there was some way to capture the *what the fuck* looks these assholes got on their faces. Every time it was the same. When the easy mark they had targeted to rob, rape, stab, kill, or mug suddenly stood tall and demanded they stop with the boring diatribe and get to the action portion of the evening, they had no idea what to do. All their threatening witticisms dried up and they stood there with their mouths open in shock, looking like fish out of water.

She sighed and threw her hands up in the air in a clear sign of frustration. "Come on, boys, I don't have all night, and I am getting sick of standing in this godforsaken alley. Y'all might be used to the smell of rotting garbage and urine, but me? Not so much. Now, I wore this butt ugly woolen coat to look all non-threatening and an easy mark for thugs like you." Violet shrugged the offending garment off, and let it fall at her feet, revealing the fight suit she wore beneath it, complete with a whole arsenal of weapons. "God, that thing was heavy. I even put on some fake glasses." Violet took them off and threw them off to the side. "They really sold the act, didn't they? But you want to know what really gets me angry? The part of this evening that is going to make what I do to the three of you a whole lot more painful than I might have otherwise, is the fact I opted to stick with my own boots."

Violet stuck her foot out and sighed at the sight of the sludge and some kind of dark goop she knew she never wanted to know what it actually was marring the side of the chunky heel of the knee-high boots she wore. "The shoes I was going to wear were *fugly* as sin, and I just couldn't bring myself to wear them, and now my beautiful kickass boots have shit on them that I am pretty sure would turn my stomach if I knew what it actually was. And that pisses me off more than you could ever imagine, and the only ones here that I can take my rage out on, are you three assholes. So I say again, enough with the talking. Pull on your big boy panties." Violet reached behind her and gripped the handles of her custom made fighting batons, pulled them from the two sheaths built into the back of her suit and spun them on the palm of her hands. "And come get some."

Chapter Two

"Christ, Mason, would you slow the fuck down?"

Mason didn't alter his stride, but he did turn to glare at his brother over his shoulder, wondering why the hell their mother hadn't drowned the bastard when they were just cubs. "Jacob, I swear to all that is holy, I'm going to rip you to pieces. If our intel is correct, then the woman Kieran told us to find might be in the alley up ahead, and she's in trouble. If you don't move your ass I'll fucking cut you."

Jacob snarled as he jogged to catch up. "Fuck you, Mason, you'd have to catch me first, and we all know who's faster."

"Only in your human form," Mason muttered under his breath, conscious that there were humans on the streets around them and he didn't want them to hear the two of them arguing. "When we run as leopards, I own your ass."

Jacob rolled his eyes in that annoying way younger brothers had. Mason and Jacob took their role as Black Ridge Enforcers seriously. They had worked their way through the ranks to earn the right to stand at their Alpha's side, but sometimes Mason just wanted to slap Jacob upside the head, and to be fair he did that often. He knew tonight that would only start a brawl and they would never make it to the woman Kieran said could help them.

They'd had to bury Jason and Vernon the day before, and the pride had yet to grieve their loss properly. Now Jacob and Mason were out in the streets, desperately looking for some kind of genius who they were told could help them. There were many enemies on the streets of Chicago, but there were friends as well.

Kieran had told them about a woman who had helped many of the victims of Santiago's tyranny. A woman who, according to a few of their allies, had access to a laboratory or team of scientists who could help with the bullets Santiago had fabricated.

Mason was also pissed off about the fact that before they'd left the house, they'd received another transmission from the group calling themselves IEH. The message was clear. The group called for all of Chicago to stand up against Santiago and take back their city. Although Mason agreed with the sentiment, the retaliation from Santiago and his group of merry fuck ups would be swift and severe.

"Come on, Mason," Jacob wheedled. "We are heading in the right damn direction. I just want you to scent the air, and tell me if you can catch the scent that is driving my leopard crazy."

Mason pushed away the anger that came with his train of thought and growled at his brother as they rounded the corner, and they were only a few feet from the entrance to the alleyway they had been directed to. "Jacob, I promise, as soon as we save this woman, I'll inhale so deep my goddamn nose will bleed, but right now I need you on the same fucking page so that we can find this woman. The informant said she was calling out for help. We need to get to her and take care of the three assholes that are stalking her!"

The two of them stepped quickly into the alley and slammed to a stop. The scene that met them was so unexpected he blinked slowly a couple of times to check that what he was seeing was in fact real. A tall curvy female with long curly red hair was putting a beating on two men, who were both swearing and cursing at her, while she swung two lethal looking fighting batons with unerring accuracy.

The two men were wielding knives and threatening the woman with each step. If anything she seemed to be amused by their threats, and if Mason wasn't mistaken, she was enjoying the hell out of the fight. Mason stepped forward when he saw the two bastards strike out at the same time, and one of them managed to connect with her upper arm. The woman frowned, and looked down at the leather that Mason could see was now wet with her blood.

"You son of a bitch," the woman muttered. "I fucking *hate* sewing. So now, despite all the fun I am having, I'm going to have to end our little dance so I can go take care of it. Which is a shame because I was just starting to think we might have something building between us." The woman then started moving with lethal intent, and Mason admired the skill and speed with which she moved. She—

"*Mate*," Jacob suddenly growled, his eyes glowing amber as his leopard drew closer to the surface.

Mason frowned as he tilted his head into the air, inhaled then almost dropped to the ground. Beneath the usual stench of an inner city alley that some obviously mistook as a public restroom, the alluring scent of cinnamon and honey hit him right in the chest. His entire body hummed with recognition of the woman the fates had deemed theirs, and he had to hold himself in check to avoid losing his shit and allowing his leopard to leap out into the open.

Once he had his equilibrium back and the shock and wonder of finding what few of their kind ever did eased, he saw their mate land a killing blow to the temple of the last man standing. His leopard growled in pleasure as they watched him drop to the ground like a proverbial rock. He didn't get back up.

The woman moved with fluid grace to face them,

her body crouched in a fighting stance that told him their mate was well trained, batons at the ready, one above her head and one pointing in their direction. She looked up at him and Jacob, and Mason's blood heated. She was stunning. She had a figure that a man could get lost in for hours and still not get enough of. Her lips were full, and her unusual almond shaped eyes were such a dark blue in color they were almost purple. If this was the woman Kieran sent them to find, then Mason was pretty sure he wouldn't be letting her go any time soon.

"Are you two friends with these assholes?" She pointed at the men at her feet. "If so, give me one minute and I'll be sure to reunite you with them."

Jacob stepped forward, holding his hands out in a non-threatening manner. "No, ma'am, we would never be friends with the likes of those two."

The woman indicated to the side with a quick flick of her head. "Three. I tossed one of them in that dumpster for calling me the 'c' word. I can live with many insults, but that one really gets my blood boiling." She relaxed out of the fighting stance she had been standing in, twirled the batons in the palms of her hands in an impressive show of expertise before she slid them into some kind of holster behind her. "Well, there is nothing left to see here. If you two aren't with these corpses, then my job here is done." She lifted her left foot and wiped her boot on the last man she'd dropped, then repeated the move with her other foot.

"Nice boots," Mason said with a grin, completely taken with the kickass woman in front of him. The fact that their mate grinned back and flicked him an air kiss in response told him that the Fates had definitely chosen well. Any woman destined to be mated to two feline shifters had to be strong, but one that was mated to protectors for their people, she needed to be able to kick ass and hold her own.

Once she had finished she stepped over the two men and walked in their direction. As she neared, her eyes lightened dramatically in a way that would have normally suggested she was shifter, but neither he nor his cat scented an animal within her. He shared a quick confused glance with his brother. She stopped ten feet from them.

"Well, now, this is a first for me," their mate said in a tone filled with curiosity. "I know of your kind of course, I mean Kieran and the feline shifters here in Chicago are infamous on the grapevines of the underbelly, right? They battle against Santiago and his douchebags and bring justice to the streets, and I for one often wondered if Kieran and his men wore their underwear on the outside?" She glanced down, and if Mason wasn't mistaken there was disappointment in her tone when she spoke again. "Alas, I see the superhero analogy dies tonight, and I do think there might be a movie deal in that story somewhere. But I have never had the pleasure of meeting a shifter in person. And now look at me, standing in an alley with not one, but two of them."

Mason tensed. "And how would you know of such things, little one?"

Their mate smiled sweetly at them, but it never reached her eyes, eyes that had returned to all their natural beauty. "Let's just say I know a lot about a lot of things, and a little about some, and mostly nothing about crap I don't give a shit about. You are both feline, so it would stand to reason that you would be a part of Kieran's what … crew? Pack? Herd? Whatever you want to call yourselves. Either way, I figure you take out the baddies, and I take out the baddies, so win-win and we are all on the same side. So," Mason watched in amazement as she dropped into a bow, one leg straight in front of her, one bent behind, and used her hand to take off an imaginary cap and waved it around like something from The Musketeers, before standing tall once more. "I bid you gentlemen *adieu* and of course, good hunting."

She spun around and moved toward the back of the alley, and Mason shared another shocked look with his brother before he gathered enough of his wits to actually move forward. "Hey wait!"

"No can do, kitty cat," their mate called back with a wave, not even slowing her stride. "I got places to be and baddies to kill, and eventually, a piece of homemade lasagna waiting for me at home that I plan to match with a nice glass of Chianti."

Mason sped up, reaching for her arm to turn her around to face them, but he never made contact. She dropped down and out of his range before he made contact, and now she was crouched in front of them in a fighting stance once more, both fists held up in front of her. From the way her gaze flew between him and Jacob, Mason knew without a doubt that she was calculating her odds of taking them both, and no doubt planning the moves she would need to execute in order to make that happen.

"Bad kitty," she scolded, and Mason held his hands up in surrender. "You don't get to touch me unless I invite you to. The last man who did that without my consent now finds it difficult to count to ten. He used to use all his fingers. He finds that hard to do with two fingers missing from each hand."

Mason looked over at his brother, hoping he might have an idea on how to defuse the situation. Their mate looked like she was seconds away from ripping out those batons of hers a second time, and he and Jacob would be locked firmly in her crosshairs.

Jacob smiled warmly and pushed his hands into his jeans. Their mate's eyes watched the move curiously, and Mason realized his brother was smarter than he had ever given him credit for. By putting his hands in his pockets, he was making himself vulnerable and giving her a tactical advantage.

"Sounds like you taught that prick a lesson," Jason said, his grin broadening. "Tell me, why only take two fingers? If I had been there and watched some fucker put his hands on you I probably would have taken his arms first, then used them to beat him death."

Their mate smiled approvingly and stood up gracefully from her crouch, but Mason noticed that she took two steps back to give her room to defend or attack if she needed to.

"That would have worked for sure," she said with a nod. "But I wanted to make a statement, so I took the same two fingers from both hands."

"Which fingers?" Mason asked, and taking a page from his brother's play book he crossed his arms over his chest.

Their mate smiled at them, and an ache settled in Mason's chest.

"I took the middle and ring finger from each hand."

Mason held out his hand, palm down and bent those fingers down. "Why those fingers in particular?"

She laughed, and Mason had to bite back a groan of appreciation at the sound. "He was always quick to throw up the middle finger. He flipped everyone off, his boss, the public, me, and I have to say it pissed me off, so I figured by taking both, he would never be able to flip anyone the bird again."

"And his ring fingers?" Jacob asked the question that Mason had been about to.

"Well, that was just a whimsical bit of fancy for me. From now on, the only hand gesture he can make is the American Sign Language sign for *I love you.*" She held her hand up, with the two aforementioned fingers down and Mason could clearly see the sign he had been taught at some point in his life. "Poetic justice really. Especially for a sadistic son of a bitch whose idea of a good time is to hurt, bleed, rape, or kill someone. He decided that I'd make a perfect rape victim for him, and I proved him wrong."

An ice cold rage flooded through him.

"Where is he now?" Jacob asked calmly, but there was no mistaking his intent.

Violet clasped her hands beneath her chin and batted her eyelids at them. "Aww, look at you, getting all protective. There's no need. A few months later I encountered him again. He had this whole scene of vengeance planned out and everything. I had to disappoint him, and now he's way too busy being dead to be a threat to anyone."

Mason dipped his head in her direction in acknowledgement. "That's good to know, but I do see your point, and have taken note of your warning. I swear I was not trying to hold you against your will, and I eagerly await your consent to touch you in the near future." Her eyes narrowed at his tongue in cheek answer, but he simply grinned back. "And knowing that you know what we are, let me complete the introductions. My name is Mason Williams, and this is my younger brother, Jacob. As you have quite rightly ascertained, we are indeed shifters. Leopards to be exact and we have pledged our fealty to Kieran and the Black Ridge *pride.*" He stressed the word and winked at her.

"Huh, just like lions, I should have totally made that connection," the beauty muttered to herself almost absently. "Thanks, I will remember that for next time. Now, if you'll excuse me, I really do have to go. This neighborhood is good at turning its back on violence within its borders, but someone might come looking for those three assholes, and I don't plan to be anywhere near them when they do."

She moved back further into the alley. There was no exit in that direction, and the smallest building around them was three stories high. There were no fire exits to speak of, so he had no idea how their mate thought to leave in that direction.

"Where are you going, beautiful?" Jacob called out, and she simply pointed up. Mason shrugged when Jacob looked back at him in question. He had no clue what she was going to. When she reached the back of the alley, she looked up then moved around until she was in whatever spot it was she was looking for.

Mason stared up into the darkened sky, but couldn't see what the hell she was lining herself up with. "Little one, I am not sure what the hell you are about to do, but I have a feeling you are going to disappear on us. We were sent by our Alpha to find you, something that we will forever be indebted to him for. Could you tell us your name?"

She dropped her head so she could look at him for a moment, then flicked her gaze to his brother, and an assessing expression fell across her beautiful face.

Jacob chuckled. "We know what you're thinking. If you give us your name, we might be able to find you, and you are probably debating with yourself if that is something you actually want to happen. But the thing you need to understand about us, baby, is that we won't stop looking for you. Not for any other reason, than we must. If you know what we are, then you must know what a mate is to our kind."

Her eyes widened with shock, and Mason heard her quick inhalation.

"That's what you are to us, little one. Our mate," Mason said in a voice he hoped rang with the truth of his words. "As soon as we got close enough to you, and could scent you over the stench of this alley, we knew you were the one meant for us, whether you are the woman Kieran thinks you may be or not. And that means that we will be moving heaven and earth to convince you to take a chance on us. So please, before you somehow disappear into the night like a dream, could you please tell us your name."

She was still for a moment looking between him and Jacob, and Mason knew she was taking their measure. Would she trust them enough? God, he hoped so. Just when his nerves were about to snap she smiled sadly, and the hope that had begun to tentatively bloom within him, wilted.

"I do know what a mate means to your kind," she said in a shy voice that endeared her to him even further, "but I don't think I am mate material. I have a lot to do before I can even contemplate being something more than what I am." She drew a strange metal thing from behind her, and when she pressed a button it lengthened. It looked like the middle sections of a longbow.

"And what is that?" Mason asked.

She lifted the mechanism above her head, and did something that had two wires shooting out from the ends and slamming into the top of the two buildings on either side of her. From the way they locked into the side of the buildings, he knew there had to be some kind of anchor on the end of each wire.

There was a sad look in her eye that had Mason wanting to hold her. "Just a granddaughter looking for some vengeance."

He reached out a hand in her direction just as she suddenly shot straight up. The mechanical whirr of the wires winding back into the piece of equipment she held in her hand sounded loud in the alley, before they heard her grunt as she reached the top.

Mason's heart leaped to his throat at the thought of the jolt causing her to lose her grip, and he and Jacob both ran forward as if to catch her if she fell. They should have had more faith. They could see the silhouette of their mate against the night sky as she began to slide down one side of the wire to the building beside them. Mason growled when she seemed to let go of the wire and flip herself up and onto the building's roof. His leopard was prowling within him, demanding that he follow, but he had no idea how.

"Well, shit, apparently our mate is fucking related to Batman," Jacob said. The two of them stood there, hands on hips, frustration riding them both, staring up at their mate as she somehow released the hooks of the fancy thing she used to scale the building and the wires wound back into the mechanism.

"Goddamn it!" Mason roared. Without a name or a place to start their mate was effectively in the wind. Short of walking around sniffing everything and everyone with the hope of stumbling across her scent, they didn't have much to go on.

"Violet."

Mason's heart stuttered at the sound of her voice. If they were human they might not have heard it, but their shifter hearing made it easy to hear her.

"My name is Violet."

Then he knew she was gone.

"Violet," Jacob whispered her name reverently. "Well, at least we have a name."

Mason nodded. He opened his mouth to say

something, but a lump at the back of the alley caught his attention. He walked toward the back wall.

"We have three things to use to find our mate. We have her name, we have this." He picked up a heavy woolen jacket that had been on the ground, but her scent was strong on the material so he knew she had worn it. "And we have the fact that Kieran is convinced she can help us, and there are a lot of people out looking for her. We put all that together and we'll find our mate."

Jacob grinned, determination shone in his eyes. "Then we will work on that whole getting her to accept us thing you were talking about. And no matter what her objections, we won't give up."

Mason turned to walk out of the alleyway, ignoring the bodies his mate had left lying on the ground, and with an excitement for the future he had never had before. "Too damn right we won't."

Chapter Three

"Three of our men have been killed on the streets tonight, boss," Matteo spoke from the door to his office, but Roberto Santiago didn't even deign to look up from the report he was reading.

He'd known Murphy would retaliate, and it was no surprise that he'd taken three lives in return for the two Santiago's men had taken. But the difference between him and the shifter was that Roberto didn't give a shit. He was completely unmoved by the deaths of three of his men. The creation of every empire that ever existed in the world came at a price. He considered the loss collateral damage on the path to fulfilling his destiny.

"Do we know who killed them?" he asked the question, but the answer didn't matter to him. Not really.

"No, boss, but their injuries were not consistent with an animal attack. These were blunt force trauma from a cylindrical object."

Roberto nodded. "Then it was that vigilante red-headed woman again. God, spare me from people who think they can save the world." He picked up a pen and began to take notes on the pad beside him. They had no real idea who she was. They had witness reports that mentioned long red curly hair, but nothing else. Not much to go on really. Roberto knew it was no coincidence that the CCV cameras were always out in the areas where she struck. He knew she was smart and had resources at her disposal, and Roberto didn't know what he wanted more, her death or her loyalty. Conviction like that was hard to find nowadays.

"Tell the boys I've added an incentive. Fifty grand to the person who brings me proof they ended that bitch." If she was that determined to save the world, turning her would be too damn difficult.

"Will do, boss." Matteo hesitated for a moment. "One more thing, our contact at the city council called."

Now this did have Roberto looking up. Matteo stood with one foot out the door, and if he was that nervous about this particular update then it did not bode well.

"And what did they have to say?" Roberto kept his voice calm despite the fact rage was building within him at a phenomenal rate.

"The contract has been awarded to IEH," Matteo said quickly.

"*Figlio di puttana*!" Roberto roared as he stood and swept the blotter and phone off his desk to the floor. "That fucking company is starting to piss me off! They write shit about me, and get it on every damn local media source in the city, they win contracts out from under me, and it feels like every time I turn around they are fucking me over. They have cost me millions, and no one can tell me who the fuck they are. Goddamn it!"

A man in the shadows at the side of the room moved slightly into the light, but not enough to be completely visible, and a wave of unease skittered over Roberto's skin. He may be the boss of one of the largest organized crime syndicates in the America, but even he answered to someone. And the man scared the shit out of him.

"Do you have control of this city or not, Roberto?" The calm voice belied the reactions Santiago had witnessed from the man in the past. Vincent Caruso was the head of the Syndicate, whatever he said was gospel, and while it was an honor to have him here in Chicago, it was embarrassing that he was here to witness this failure firsthand.

"I have control," Santiago said adamantly. "There

are a couple of speed bumps, but we will overcome them, I promise you."

Vincent made a noise of disbelief. "You will of course forgive me for my misgivings. I see this IEH time and again in your reports, but still no information into who is behind it. I get the odd report that there is a woman laying waste to some of your men in random alleyways, and again, no reports on who she is. And then you know there is the Black Ridge issue. There is a plague in this city, led by Kieran Murphy, and despite my wishes, that man is still breathing, so it is very hard for me to believe you when you say you have things under control."

Santiago felt a vein begin to pulse at his temple. He was not used to being mocked, or questioned, and it burned to have to listen to what Caruso had to say. "I understand your reservations, but there is a plan in play. We have a weapon against the shifters, one that cost me a small fortune, but makes it easier to remove them from the equation. The redhead is no threat to us. She keeps to the streets, and removes some of our more impatient and unskilled men, and as far as I am concerned they are easily replaced and no real loss to what we are planning. Chicago is ours."

Vincent stood and walked out of the shadows. The thousand dollar suit the man wore screamed affluence, but the dark, soulless eyes told a much deadlier story. "We have the ability to transport our product and run the business the way we want, but we need the city officials behind us. Either through the political and financial strength we can offer through legitimate business ventures or through extortion. The latter comes with too much risk. We need to gain those contracts and lift the legitimate profile of our business."

Santiago resisted the urge to snap at the man who

was for all intent and purposes his boss. "We will. IEH is a blip, but it is one that we can overcome."

Caruso raised a sardonic eyebrow. "That remains to be seen. This IEH, they love this city. They love the people in the city, and they think that somehow they will be able to convince the spineless hordes to stand up against your tyranny, just like the redhead. Perhaps there is a connection? Or at the very least, her very public death would send a strong message."

"True," Roberto said thoughtfully. "Then we strike back at the city and the people themselves. If we are lucky, we'll get the opportunity to remove more of that damn pride, but this time, we make it very clear that we do so because of IEH." He pushed the button on his phone that would connect him immediately to Matteo. "Find that red-headed bitch and bring her to me."

****

"No mention of the three dead scumbags in a back alley," Violet mumbled to herself as she reached for her coffee cup. "No surprises there."

Violet sat at the kitchen table in her loft, reading through the papers and generally taking her time before she started her day. She had slept in that morning so the day was beginning later than normal, but she hadn't slept very well. She could lie to herself and say that it had something to do with the fact that she had killed three men last night, but that didn't really have anything to do with it.

Of course, Violet understood that killing was wrong. But for fucktards like the three who had pushed her into that alleyway last night with the intent to rape and scar her for life she had no hesitation. Furthermore, she felt no remorse for her actions. Santiago and his organization had filled this city with every lowlife, murdering scumbag the bastard had ever met. Just as it said in that open letter the city woke up to this morning, her actions had been about eradicating an infestation. And she was just the exterminator for the job.

No, it wasn't guilt that had kept her awake last night. It was the thought of two leopard shifters that had kept her tossing and turning all night. Mason was the older of the two, and Violet knew immediately that he was the more serious. He was taller than she was by quite a bit, and she guessed he stood about six foot four. His dark blond hair was cut short at the back and sides, but there was a tousled length to the top that had her fingers twitching to touch the silken strands.

Jacob was the softer of the two, which was almost crazy to think, but that was the impression she got. The man stood just as tall as his brother, and only slightly smaller in build, but he was the one who had approached her slowly, not wanting to scare her, and she had to appreciate that. His hair was wavy, and fell almost to the collar of the black shirt he was wearing the night before, and she wondered if it was as soft as it looked.

Sighing she stood up from the table and moved into the kitchen to put away her breakfast things. The brothers were the reason for her late start. Her sleep had been filled with dreams of the two men. Erotic dreams that had her waking up hot and needy a few times, and on one occasion she awoke to cry out her release as she came from the erotic things they did to her in her dream, only to growl in frustration to find that she was alone.

"Come on, Violet," she scolded herself as she found herself dwelling on those dreams yet again. "Get your shit together and get into the gym."

Ten minutes later, and Violet was in her gym on the roof of the building she owned. She'd had a glass conservatory built on the roof, and it housed her gym, dojo, and sauna, and it opened out into the pool area. The building was the tallest in the neighborhood so she had no one that looked down onto her private oasis, and that was exactly how she liked it. She loved everything about the loft and rooftop she called home, but it was the gym, dojo, and pool area that pleased her most.

She finished up her warm-up, and moved toward her cardio machines. Twenty minutes on the treadmill, followed by twenty minutes on her Jacobs Ladder machine, and a final twenty on her rowing machine and she was a hot, sweaty mess. The workout had succeeded in clearing her mind, but the thought of the two shifters who had proclaimed her their mate the night before still lingered.

She stepped into the dojo and started working her way through her *kata*. She didn't have much in her life that she could thank her parents for beyond being born, but they had started her with karate lessons at a young age, and it was something she enjoyed and had excelled at. Now, it was a skill necessary for her life's work, and it was ironic that she had them to thank for it. When she was finished, her workout clothes were dripping wet, but she definitely felt more centered.

After a shower she threw on some yoga pants, a tank top, and a loose shirt and headed into her office. A quick glance at the clock on the wall and she saw that it was almost lunchtime. Grabbing a bottle of water from the fridge built into the cabinets at the side of the room, she sat down at her desk in front of the three large flat screens, and pressed a button on the keyboard in front of her. The center monitor came to life instantly.

"Morning, V!" A cheery voice sounded through the speakers, just as the image of a woman in her fifties, hair piled into a bun on the top of her head opened on her screen.

Violet smiled. "Morning, Dot, how are you on

this fine day?" Dot was her secretary and her friend and one of the few people in the world Violet trusted. She had been working for Violet for the past five years, and Dot had proven her loyalty to her on more than one occasion.

"Oh, I'm fine, sweets, nothing to worry about here." Dot grinned into the camera. "My Johnny still thinks I have the best job in the world, and I have to agree. Not many women my age get to work from home, earn an impressive salary and get asked to fly around the world to meet with businessmen and -women on behalf of her employer."

"Speaking of which." Violet grabbed a folder from the desk beside her, then ran the papers in it through the scanner. "I am sending you information on the next trip I would like you to make if you wouldn't mind."

"Ooo, adventure time!" Dot almost sang, and Violet laughed. "Where am I going now? Is it somewhere new?"

Violet nodded into the screen loving how Dot's eyes lit up in excitement. "Yep! This time I need you to head over to Wellington, New Zealand. I have been in communication with the head of information systems for their Ministry of Education. They have some issues with the national processing system that pays their teachers, and I have a solution. They want to see my program at work in house so to speak."

Dot nodded as she grabbed the papers from the scanner identical to Violet's on the desk beside her. "That sounds like something you would enjoy. Going in and fixing someone else's mistakes, it's more fun for you if there is a problem attached."

"Ah, you think you know me so well," Violet teased, reveling in the older woman's chuckle. "Now, I want you to take that husband of yours and stay over there for a couple of weeks."

Dot's expression turned serious, and she moved closer to the camera on her laptop. "We have to get ready to deliver phase one of what we proposed to the Chicago City Council. Why are you sending me halfway around the world? You only send me and hubby out of the country if you think there might be trouble heading our way through your other … endeavors."

Violet winced as her ever astute secretary hit the nail on the head. "Last night didn't exactly go as planned."

"What happened? Are you hurt? Do you need me to come to you? I can be on a flight to Chicago in an hour and be at your place in less than four."

And that right there was why Violet loved Dot so much. She would drop anything and run head long into danger if she thought Violet was in trouble.

"No, I'm not hurt, I'm fine." Violet thought it best not to mention the three stitches she'd had to put in her own arm to sew up the wound one of the bastards had managed to score on her last night. "Don't come here. It is safer for you to stay exactly where you are."

"Then why are you sending me halfway around the world and insisting that I take my Johnny with me?"

Violet sighed and decided to go with the truth. "On my patrol last night I came across two men who turned up just as I finished dispatching a couple of douche-knuckles."

Dot knew everything about her, and was completely behind her nocturnal activities. She and Johnny had lived in Chicago for many years, raising their two sons. Both of whom had been officers in the Chicago Police Department and had been killed at the hands of Santiago's men, and on his direct orders.

"Who were they? What did they want?"

"Mason and Jacob Williams. They are two of

Kieran's men," Violet said.

Dot had gone quiet, which for her was never a good thing, and Violet peered into the screen. Dot's expression was … gleeful. Yes, gleeful that was the word for how the woman looked in this moment. "Why do you look like that?"

"I'm not sure if you noticed, sweetling, but your tone completely changed when you mentioned their names," Dot said with a grin, and Violet felt a heat rise into her cheeks in the first blush she'd had since she was an awkward teenager. "Are you blushing? You are, aren't you? Ha! I knew it! These shifters you met were hot and sexy and they got your girly parts all tingly, didn't they?"

"Dot!" Violet exclaimed, never having heard her speak about girly parts, tingly or otherwise.

"Tell me I'm wrong?" Dot paused, and Violet remained stoically silent. "You can't, can you? Because you think they're hot. You met two shifters last night in a dark alley, and they left an impression on you. Oh, I thought this would never happen!" Dot clapped her hands and rubbed them together. "I might get me some grandbabies after all! Wait, would that make them grandkittens?"

"Stop it, old lady, or I will fire your ass," Violet said through her laughter. "You've gone crazy. Johnny is loving you up and making you crazy, and I—"

A beeping sound from the screen to her left as it suddenly blinked to life and the vibration of her watch against her wrist had her stopping midsentence. She turned her attention to the screen. It was split into four separate images. The top left was car park level of the private elevator that led to her loft, and the one next to that was inside the elevator itself. The two at the bottom were different angles of the foyer downstairs where her building security screened everyone who came into the building.

The alarm had sounded because something about the two men who were standing in front of the front desk had concerned the guard. He was well trained, and Violet could count on one hand the number of times he had used this alert. She flicked one of the views to the camera behind the guard to get a look at the two men, and inhaled sharply.

"What is it?" Dot asked. She had heard the alarm sound but had kept quiet in order to give Violet time to assess the situation.

Violet frowned and took a deep breath. "Mason and Jacob have found me."

"What! How in the hell did they manage to do that?'

Violet shrugged her shoulders. "I may have, kinda, sorta, told them my real name before I disappeared into the night."

There was a hesitation on the other end of the call. "You told them your real name?"

Violet nodded, and Dot mouthed a silent O before morphing into a grin. "Okay then, I guess there is more to the story than you're telling me. I'll call Johnny, and we'll make plans to leave according to the information you sent through. But leave your alert on, and press it if you need me to send in the cavalry. But before I go, sweetling, let me just say this. Sometimes a burden shared is a burden halved. If these guys are part of Kieran's men and were in that alleyway last night, then they already know a side of you that no one else does. Don't close yourself off from something more. Just see where things take you."

Dot was grinning like a crazed woman again, and Violet knew she had romantic notions in her head about what brought them to her doorstep. Violet would have normally shot something witty back and rolled her eyes for effect, but if the truth be told, she was kind of in shock. She nodded and closed the connection down between her and Dot, then turned the sound up on the scene downstairs.

"I'm sorry, sir," the guard was explaining, "but for the third time, without a last name or a security clearance word that the person you are looking for may have supplied you with, I cannot call upstairs and nor can I allow you past this point."

"That's actually a really smart security measure," Mason said as he leaned on the counter. "It is one that I can not only understand, but we will probably steal and implement in some of the properties our extended family own—" by that Violet knew he meant the pride, "—but if you could simply let Ms. Violet know that Mason and Jacob are here, and that we won't be leaving anytime soon, we would be most grateful. In fact, we are more than happy to sit outside and wait for her to come home so we may speak with her."

Jacob leaned in to match his brother's position and leaned on the counter. "Tell her that she has no reason to fear us. Surely she's not scared of little old us?" Violet chuckled at that, as did the security guard. "True, we do outweigh her by a lot, but I happen to know she can hold her own. But hey, maybe she just doesn't have the nerve to talk with us."

Violet tensed at the challenge in Jacob's tone. Could he know that she was listening to him?

Son of a cheese whip covered cracker.

"I think that's exactly what it is, brother," Mason said as his eyes shot to the camera, so it looked like he was staring directly at her from the screen. "She's scared about what we told her last night, and what she means to us."

Jacob's eyes lifted to the same camera, and the half smile and challenging lift of one brow had her own brow rising. "Well, damn. Maybe we need to think about our immediate impression. Perhaps she's not as fearless as we thought."

They were deliberately trying to goad her into speaking to them. They were employing the oldest and most childish trick in the book to lure her to engage, and goddamn it all to hell and back, it was working.

Violet muttered to herself as she reached for the cordless phone beside her and pressed the pound key. She watched as both the shifters expressions turned hopeful and the guard grinned as he picked up the phone, knowing it was her immediately. "Yes, ma'am?"

"Aren't they assholes, Reggie? Standing there and freaking calling me out like that," Violet complained down the phone. Reggie had worked there for the past three years and knew she owned the building, but they had never met face to face, only ever talked via the phone.

"That they are, ma'am. What would you like me to do with them?" Reggie stared at Mason and Jacob with a huge grin on his face and Mason and Jacob both tried to grab the phone off him at the same time, but he pushed his chair back with a laugh. "I could throw them out if you want, ma'am, just say the word."

"Jeez, dude," Jacob complained pressing a hand to his chest. "That's fucking cold. We're here on a mission of love and you'd throw us out on our ass?"

Reggie covered the phone, but Violet could hear his answer clearly through the monitor. "In a heartbeat. That woman is the best boss a man could have, and she has a huge heart. Me and my Virginia both work for her here, and she pays us well, and takes care of everyone who works for her. If I thought you'd hurt her, or if she wanted nothing to do with either of you, I'd throw you out on your ass just as soon as look at ya."

Violet's jaw dropped. She knew that Reggie and Virginia were married, but she'd never known that they felt so protective of her.

"Thank you, Reggie," Mason said solemnly, nodding at the older man now standing behind the desk. "You've been looking out for our woman when we haven't been here to do it. We will never hurt Violet. If we do, then you have my permission to shoot Jacob in the leg. Twice."

"Yeah, we would nev—wait. What! Asshole," Jacob muttered as he shook his head at his brother, and Violet giggled again. The sound brought Reggie's attention back to the phone.

"Sorry, ma'am, just clearing something up with your visitors. What would you like me to do?"

Violet took a deep breath and released it slowly. "Send them up, Reggie."

And just like that, Violet felt a shift in her world. Only time would tell if the shift was to be a positive one, or something that ended in her blood being spilt, just like it usually did.

Chapter Four

Jacob was a bundle of nerves as the elevator sped them up from the ground floor. The foyer had two elevators against the far wall, and then a third, private elevator just off to the side of the security desk. Reggie sent them to the private elevator, and Jacob and Mason had shared a pointed look. There was only one button in the elevator so he knew that it led directly to her apartment. When the trail to find their mate led them to this building, he and Mason had stood outside for a long time, taking in the beauty of the building itself.

It was twenty stories high, and typical of some of architecture Chicago was famous for. With its clearly gothic in style, decorative patterns, scalloping and lancet windows, it was a truly beautiful building.

From the not so legal information gathering task one of their Black Ridge pridemates had conducted a short while ago, they had found the property was owned by a company called Hyacinthinum. The company itself had real estate interests all over the city, but what set this building apart from all the rest, was the fact that the top two floors, and the rooftop were owned by one person, and they had struggled to find the name. What had Mason convinced they were in the right place was the fact that Hyacinthinum was the Latin word for Violet.

The elevator dinged as they reached their destination, and the doors opened to reveal the open plan penthouse apartment. Where at first glance it looked like the entire floor was open plan, Jacob could see that one end of the building did in fact have a wall. Along that wall was a huge galley style kitchen with a large granite kitchen island that looked like it could be featured on the cover of a magazine. There was a large dining table at one side, where diners could look out over the city all the way to the water, and a comfortable looking seating area with huge fireplace and flat screen TV that looked cozy and inviting.

Jacob would have liked to continue looking around, but his gaze suddenly landed on the woman standing on the other side of the room, just behind a curved, cast iron staircase that obviously led to the roof. Violet was staring at them between the stairs, her gaze curious and pensive.

"Hey, baby," Jacob called out, and stepped further into the room. "Thanks for letting us come up and talk with you."

Mason stepped in with him, but neither of them crossed too far into her space, not until she invited them to. "We thought you might refuse to see us, and then we'd have to camp out on your building's doorstep and that might drop the value of your property if we did that for too long."

Violet gave them a small smile then stepped out from behind the staircase. Jacob's breath caught in his throat at how soft and beautiful she looked in what she was wearing. She had on a pair of loose black pants that sat low on her hips and a black tank top that finished just above the waistline of her pants and left an alluring strip of white skin bare at her midriff when she moved. She wore a loose, see-through white top that finished just below her breasts, and swung loosely down her arms to her elbows. Her hair was pulled up on her head in a twist thing that left tendrils falling softly on either side of her face.

"Well, I don't know about that. If people knew you could turn into huge house trained cats, I think they might see that as beneficial," she said dryly as she padded in their direction, her arms crossed loosely at her waist. "This is a surprise. I know I gave you my name last night, but that shouldn't have gotten you anywhere near me. How did you find me?

Mason huffed a quick laugh. "You left your subway ticket in your pocket."

Violet closed her eyes and shook her head in a self-depreciating way. "Rookie mistake."

"But one I am most thankful for," Jacob insisted. "We were able to track you from your station, and then it was a matter of following our noses. Literally."

Violet frowned. "So what, you walked around smelling everything until you struck upon my particular flavor of stank?"

"No!" Mason was quick to say. "But yeah, kinda. Your scent is unique to us, and had it been any other shifters looking for you it would have been impossible to find you. But for Jacob and me, with the incentive we had, it was slightly easier. Hard, but not impossible. We searched the neighborhood all night and found the building a couple of hours ago."

Violet looked at them both for a moment then smiled. "I'm impressed. Come on in and have a seat. Tell me what you're doing here."

Jacob moved into the living area, and waited until Violet had taken a seat on one of the large arm chairs, tucking her legs up under her in a feminine way that had his dick swelling. He sat down on the couch near her quickly, in an effort to hide the visual signs of his arousal. *Christ!* He had to get control of himself.

"There are a couple of reasons, but the first I would have thought that was obvious?" Mason said as he sat on the chair opposite Jacob so that they were on either side of their mate. "We told you who and what you are to us, and that we need to be near you to protect you."

Her brow shot up. "Really?" she said in a dry tone. "I am pretty sure my actions last night proved to you that I don't need any one man, or two shifters, or any number of anyone protecting me. I can do that myself."

Jacob nodded. "Without doubt. But when we met you last night a connection formed that for us means everything. Can you tell us that you felt nothing … because I don't think you can?" Jacob held his breath as Violet seemed to assess what he was saying. He only breathed again when she didn't say anything.

"You felt the bond between us, too, didn't you, little one?" Mason asked quietly.

Their mate crossed her arms and leveled Mason with a look. "Now, why would you think that, kitty cat?"

"Because we're pretty damn sure you're more than what you appear," Mason answered. "Last night, you knew with nothing more than a look that we were shifters. Two of the elders in our pride told us of people who have a psychic ability more heightened than most, and includes the gift of being able to read auras. And we reckon that ability makes it easier for you to sense the bond. Our aura is decidedly feline, for obvious reasons, and your eyes lightened when you walked toward us. You were reading us, weren't you?"

It was a statement and not a question, but their mate nodded anyway. "You can't blame a girl for checking to see the type of person she thought she was about to throw down with."

"You do that with everyone you fight?"

She threw Jacob a scowl at his question. "Of course I do! I would never risk fighting with, hurting, or killing anyone that didn't deserve it. When a person is intrinsically evil, and their actions in life are fundamentally malevolent, it leaves a mark on them. It may not affect their personality, and hell, they may be the kind of sadistic asshole who enjoys it, but it leaves a stain on their aura." Jacob watched as their mate's expression turned glacial. "It darkens, and becomes toxic, and when you reach out to them, to sense if that toxicity is a result of their actions or their environment, you get flashes of what they've done, or what's been done to them, and it affects you."

Violet's voice was a mere whisper now, and Jacob couldn't stay where he was. He shoved off the couch at the same time Mason left his chair and both of them were instantly crouched before their mate, each of them clasping one of her little hands in theirs. Jacob's heart jumped at the jolt of recognition that shot through him at the touch, but the joy of that was eclipsed by his concern at how cold her hand was.

"You see through their eyes, and the joy or excitement or, God forbid, the arousal they feel in the moment they hurt or kill someone," Violet's breath caught for a moment, and she inhaled sharply through her nose, "becomes yours for that moment you are in contact."

Mason growled low in his chest. "Then don't do it. I can see that it is taking a toll on you, little one."

Violet pulled her hands free and glared at Mason. "And what, Mason? Just leave them to it, and let them keep hurting innocent people, and selling them into the sex trade? You have to know that's what they are doing, right? No, I can't do that. And as for it hurting me, how could it not be? I can't see my own aura. I can only see the auras of those around me. But, with all the hideous things I have seen, the pain and suffering I have inflicted, I have to ask what that is doing to *my* aura?"

Jacob leaned up and pressed a quick kiss to Violet's cheek, shocking her slightly if her quick gasp was anything to go by. "Your aura is perfect, blemish free and beautiful." Jacob pretended to think about that for a moment. "Well, maybe not completely blemish free, you *are* cheeky and sarcastic as hell, and I'm sure that's left a slight smudge or two on your aura." Violent smiled like he meant her to, and she wrinkled her nose in the cutest damn way. "We know what Santiago and his bastards do, and there is not a day that goes by where we aren't thinking of some way to put a stop to it all. But none of that shit can touch you, because no matter what you see in the evil you fight, or the fact that you take those fuckers out of this world kicking and screaming, none of it can outweigh the good that you do, and the innocents you save. There is nothing in this world that could convince me otherwise."

Violet's smile broadened, and he saw that it finally reached her eyes. His heart swelled at how beautiful she was. She bit her bottom lip before she leaned in to press a kiss to his cheek. Now, Jacob was a smart leopard, and he never let an opportunity pass him by, so as soon as she was about to press her lips to his cheek, he turn his head quickly and caught her lips with his.

She pulled back with a gasp, and lifted a hand to press them to her lips as she stared at him, her eyes filled with wonder and a decent amount of lust that had his own arousal spiraling out of control. Exercising more control than he knew he had, he held still, waiting to see what she did next, hoping that she didn't haul back and slug him, and praying at the same time that she leaned in one more time for a better, longer, and more satisfying kiss.

Just as he was about to pull back and give her room, convinced that he had taken things too far, too soon, she leaned in and placed her lips on his again. There was no hesitation or instant withdrawal this time. She opened her mouth, and he moaned as her tongue slid along the seam of his lips. Then he swooped in and took control, his tongue sliding in over hers, and he claimed her mouth with his own.

****

Violet was stunned by her own courage for a split second, not knowing what possessed her to lean in for another kiss, or where she found the courage to run her tongue over the seam of his lips, but she did. Then when he groaned against her and took control of the kiss, she could do nothing more than to wrap her arms up around his shoulders and hang on. Jacob took her mouth completely, staking his claim in such a sensual way that Violet felt her entire body soften, and heat began to pool between her legs.

Jacob pressed a bite to her bottom lip, and Violet moaned when he swiped his tongue against it as if to remove the sting. How was he to know it was the sting that had her pressing her legs together? She heard a growling noise coming from behind her over the pounding of her own heart. Jacob pulled back slightly and placed a few soft kisses to her swollen lips. When the growling seemed to swell within the room, Jacob grinned.

"Baby, I think my brother is feeling a little left out," Jacob said in a voice that sounded suspiciously smug in that moment.

Violet turned to face Mason, still wrapped in Jacob's arms, and she had no recollection of when he'd done that. Mason was leaning over the arm of the chair, his eyes on her. She ran her tongue over her bottom lip, and Mason's gaze dropped immediately to track its movements. Her heart rate and breathing had been slowly returning to normal now that Jacob had stopped kissing her, but the sight of Mason's desire for her was enough to throw her right back to where she started, her heart pounding a rapid beat within her chest, and drawing in air faster than she normally would.

"Come to me, little one." Mason's voice was a growl, but Violet heard the plea in his tone. She smiled loving that his gray eyes shifted to an amber color right in front of her and she knew that was his leopard.

She pulled gently out of Jacob's arms, and reached up to cup Mason's face in the palms of her hands. She tilted her head as she approached him, and just to draw the moment out she hesitated a mere hair's breadth from making contact. Her gaze locked with his, and she felt the intensity of that look in every cell of her body.

If anyone were to ask her who moved forward first, Violet couldn't say. Perhaps they moved in unison, but in an instant their mouths were pressed together and she was being claimed once more. Or at least that was how it felt to her. Mason seemed to surge up so that he could lean down over her, lifting his own hands to her neck and tilting her head with his thumbs to the angle he wanted. She slid her hands from his face to grip his hips, and simply held on for the ride.

Where Jacob's kiss was a building domination, one that started gentle until out of nowhere he consumed her, Mason was more direct. His claim was instant and complete, and the way he tilted her head gently to the angles he wanted was so damn hot, her body released a flood of hot liquid, and from the growls of approval that filled the room around her she knew they could scent her arousal on the air. In shock and more than a little embarrassed, Violet pulled away with a cry, putting the back of her hand against her mouth.

"Little one?" Mason asked. He hadn't moved, and from the look of guilt on his face, Violet knew he thought she'd scared her.

"I'm okay," she whispered, "just a little surprised

at myself."

Jacob reached out and gently drew her hand away from her mouth. "Why, baby?"

Violet took a deep breath and decided to be honest rather than resort to her usual sarcastic defense. "I'm not usually this easy. I am not the type of girl to simply throw herself at a man, let alone two. I have no idea what came over me. You must think I'm a slut."

Mason reached out to gently turn her face toward him. "Where the hell is that coming from? Violet, the mating bond that snapped into place for us the moment we caught your scent, is not just one way. In that moment, we connected to you on a level that no other human being in the world ever could. The connection probably affects you more because of your heightened abilities."

Violet frowned as she thought about that for a moment. "So these feelings, it's like a chemical reaction thing?"

Jacob chuckled as he lifted her hand to his mouth and placed a nibbling kiss against her knuckles that had her drawing in a quick breath. "That would be the easiest answer for you, now wouldn't it, baby? But no, it's not just a chemical thing, although I think I speak for all of us when I say that we have off the fucking charts chemistry. No, the connection just identifies the other half of our soul. That's you. The speed at which the attraction has built between us, and the need we have for each other, that's very, *very* real."

Mason reached out and placed a hand on her knee, and Violet could feel the heat of his hand through the fabric of her pants. "What had you pulling away from me before?" Violet hesitated for a moment. "If it was because I was coming on too strong then just tell me."

Violet was shaking her head before he had even

finished speaking. "No, I was enjoying everything, but I pulled back because it must have been extremely obvious to you both just how *much* I was enjoying it." The brothers shared another confused look, then turned back to her, and she rolled her eyes. "Good lord! You have to learn how to read between the damn lines. I embarrass too damn easily for the two of you to be completely oblivious to what I am saying. Christ, get a damn clue. How the hell is this supposed to work as anything like a relationship if you cannot understand what I am saying to you?" Violet slumped back in her chair with a pout, her arms crossed over her chest.

Mason grinned at her. "You are so fucking cute when you pout. Little one, Jacob and I promise to work on learning to speak Violet, I promise, but in the meantime take pity on us and spell this one out for us."

Violet narrowed her eyes and had to fight to keep the smile from her face. "Fine, but next time you just have to work it out. I pulled away because I felt myself … there was a moment when … I was getting turned on by it all and … grrrr!" *Why the hell can I not find the damn words?*

Jacob's smile was genuine, and understanding glittered in his eyes. "We get it now, baby. You pulled away from Mason because you were aroused, and your pussy released all that sweet, sweet honey and you knew we could smell your arousal as it perfumed the air."

Violet's jaw dropped. "Why the hell can you say it and it sounds almost poetic, but when I try the only thing I can think to say is 'I creamed myself'?"

"I can honestly say, I preferred the way you said it," Mason said dryly.

The brothers laughed with her, and Violet realized she was completely relaxed in their presence. That never happened. Not once in the time since they had left the elevator had she run through an escape plan, or worked out what she needed to do to block an attack from either of them. She had simply sat here and listened when they talked, talked when she needed to, and let's not forget the fact that she had kissed both of them with everything in her. It was going to take her a while to process that.

"God, I wish I knew what you were thinking right now."

She looked up at Jacob's question and the curious look on his face made her smile softly, but she shook her head. "Nope, some things are for me and me alone. But I do have a question for you." She turned to look at Mason. "You said there were two reasons you wanted to see me. What's the second?"

Mason nodded, and pulled a plastic bag out of his pocket and handed it to her.

Looking down, she turned it over in her hand. "It's a forty-five millimeter round, and it could be from an M16 but is more likely to have been fired from a Beretta ARX160." She knew these rounds well, and the weapon that it came from was popular for Santiago's men. "There's blood on the round?" She looked up questioningly, and she inhaled at the sorrow she saw in their eyes.

"Yeah, we took that out of one of our pridemates yesterday," Mason said quietly, and seemed to swallow around the pain she heard in his tone. "We buried him and another one of ours straight after."

Violet's heart ached. "I am so sorry."

"Not your fault, baby," Jacob reassured her as he placed a hand on her knee. "But thank you. What you're holding is the other reason we are here. Kieran has heard that you might have the skills or ability to find out what that thing is coated with, and how it forces a shifter into a spontaneous shift." Violet eyes widened a little in shock.

"Yeah, you heard right. Whatever is on that damn thing not only drives a shifter back into their human form, but also inhibits our ability to heal, which is obviously bad for our health and affects our ability to live."

Violet smiled gently at Jacob, seeing his attempted humor for exactly what it was, something to break the tension and bring some levity to the conversation. "So, you came here to ask for my help, which I am more than happy to give. I'll look into it." Violet paused for a moment and gathered her courage to ask, "What happens now?"

"Now?" Jacob said. "I was hoping you'd have lunch with us. We'd like to spend some time with you and get to know you and allow you to get to know us. There are some things we need to discuss and at some stage our Alpha would really love the opportunity to meet you, but that doesn't have to be today. There is some urgency around the bullet though."

Violet knew she had the equipment that would be able to find out what the bullet was coated in. And if she couldn't then she'd run one of her little hacking missions into Santiago's systems.

"And the whole thing where I am your mate?" Violet asked. "What do we do about that? What am I supposed to do?"

Mason laughed gently as he leaned in and pressed a kiss to her cheek. "There is no cheat sheet for this, little one. Jacob and I have never been mated before, so we are all in the exact same boat. We just want to take the time to get to know you and for you to take the time to get to know us."

Violet smiled up at them both. "I can do that."

And she could. She would take the time to get to know them as they get to know her. She could only hope that once they got to know her, they could overlook where she came from and who she was, because not many of the people in her life ever had.

Chapter Five

An hour later, after Violet had cooked a perfect spaghetti and meatballs dish for them and Mason fell that little bit more in love with the woman, he followed her out a door he thought led to the rooftop of the building. When he stepped out into a small but well equipped gym he let out a low whistle.

"Damn, Violet, this place is awesome!" Mason wondered around, taking in the glass that surrounded the gym and the area he immediately recognized as a dojo. "This is the best damn rooftop conservatory I have ever seen."

Violet beamed with pride. "I know, right? This is my favorite part of my place. When I had them build the conservatory and they found out it was for a gym, they thought I was crazy. But it has heating and cooling with the air conditioning unit at that end, and LEDs run along the inside of the roof framing so it lights up nice in here when I want to work out at night."

Jacob walked over to the far wall and looked down over the street. "The conservatory is set back enough you can't see it clearly from the street, but you are completely out in the open if someone had a drone or a helicopter."

Mason had been so taken with the room, he hadn't thought of that, and hearing it know had his leopard snarling within him to insist that she moved everything downstairs and block off the roof access. But he was starting to get to know his mate, and he knew she had already accounted for that. "Let me guess, one way glass?"

Violet rewarded him with a sassy wink. "Something like that. A little polymer of my own invention that makes the glass impossible to see through, and before you ask, yes, it is bullet proof and the roof has cameras and sensors all over it, so no one can get to me from the roof without me knowing about it."

Mason sat down on the weight bench in the middle of the gym. "So, where do you fit into this Hyacinthinum Corporation? They own the building, and whoever's behind that business has gone to great lengths to hide the fact you are living here." Violet just looked at him. "Well, hell. You own the business don't you?"

Violet nodded as she moved to open the sliding door on the south wall and stepped out into the pool area. "I do, along with a couple of others. When I was old enough to hack into his financial systems, I took some of my grandfather's money back from the prick that took it from him. I've used that to create my own little empire that allows me to be who I am and what I am, and of course mess with Santiago as much as humanly possible."

Mason and Jacob followed her outside and walked over to where she stared into the still waters of her pool. "How old were you when you did that?"

"Fifteen," Violet's voice was flat, and Mason almost regretted asking. "My childhood was not an especially good one, not really. My parents only had me to appease my grandfather, and although he doted on me, my parents thought I was piece of shit and treated me like one. My Poppa was the only one in my life I could depend on, and who loved me for who I am."

Mason vowed to do everything he had to, to make it onto that list. "Do you think Santiago knows who you are? I mean when we talked with Kieran about you last night. He knew of a woman who matched your description who had appeared seemingly out of nowhere eighteen months ago, taking out some of Santiago's puppets, but not your name or your story. When he started asking around about someone who could help with a chemical issue we had, people mentioned you, and he worked out that you were one and the same person. He also knew you as someone who was generous to the people who saw you as a protector, and who had a reputation for making the streets a little safer."

Violet grinned, flicking a glance up at him, mirth shimmering in her eyes. "Yeah, that's me, a modern day, female Robin Hood."

"Is that why you do it?" Jacob asked.

"I do it because Santiago has gotten rich off the people in those neighborhoods for years." Violet's voice was strained. "They traffic young girls into the sex trade, and it makes me sick that all of that is taking place in my city. It pisses me off that he robs, steals, and kills anyone who dares to stand up to him and he allows his men free rein to do whatever the hell they want, to anyone they want. Just as long as *he* keeps getting more money and more power. So, yeah I do what I can to remove them from the equation."

Mason tensed. "You didn't answer my earlier question. Does he know who you are, Violet?"

****

She sighed and moved over to the outdoor daybed and sat down on it. Despite her relaxed demeanor, her mind was whirling. Did she tell them? If she answered that question truthfully, and then explained how that connection worked then everything that she had spent the last twelve years working towards and protecting would be out in the open.

"How likely is it for this mating bond to break?" Her question helped stall for time, but she had to admit she was curious as to what the answer would be.

Mason and Jacob snarled at the question, and from the amber change to their eyes, Violet knew their leopards had drawn closer to the surface. Why did that have her heart skipping a beat and her breath rate increasing?

"Why the fuck would you want us to do that?"

Violet looked up, her expression wary. "I told you both before that I am willing to get to know you, and I am telling you more about myself than anyone else knows. Christ, I have given you enough about myself that if Santiago ever found out who I was and where I live, he would crucify me. I ask because I want to know, as a shifter, is it possible to live and find love after your mate dies, or the bond is broken?"

"We would never break the damn bond," Jacob snapped, and Violet heard his leopard in his tone. "Hell, I don't think that's even possible. There has never been a case of mates breaking the bond, but there have been cases where one has passed into the next life before the others. And what happens then, Violet, is that those that are left behind follow. That is what it is to be mates."

Violet stared at the two men in shock. "You would commit suicide if I was to die? Is that what you're saying?"

Mason shook his head sadly. "We wouldn't have to. Once the bond is complete, the connection between us would be so strong that if you died, we could not survive it."

Violet couldn't comprehend an emotion that ran that deep. She had suffered loss, and she had started on this path of vengeance that she was determined to see through to the end, but devotion that deep seemed alien to her.

"What the hell is wrong with you two?" she said in a voice that was at least an octave higher than normal. "You tell me that you believe me to be your mate, then lay this on me? I will not be responsible for your deaths.

Why the hell would any woman allow that bond to be completed, if this was the inevitable outcome? When I care for someone, I do it with everything that I am. That's just the way I am. Being with you and knowing that if I were to suddenly get hit by a bus crossing the road tomorrow, you would both lose the will to live would go against that. So, find yourselves another mate!"

She stood up to stomp past them, but came to a halt when Mason wrapped his arms around her from behind, locking her own at her side. Oh, she could get free if she wanted, but the feel of being held tight in his arms did crazy things to her thought processes.

"Just hold on a minute, little one," Mason whispered behind her, and she harrumphed at the hint of joy in his voice. "You feel something for us, and that is a start. If the bond falls into place, it will be because you have accepted it and us. Calm down, love."

Despite the heat that build within her at the endearment, she struggled in his arms, albeit halfheartedly. "I am calm. I am calmly trying to decide if I shouldn't just walk into the dojo, grab my katana, and take your stupid asses out of the world. There might even be a prize for doing it."

Jacob laughed as he moved to stand in front of her, sliding the back of his fingers down her cheek and making her shiver. "We have never claimed to be smart, baby. The bond will only snap into place for the three of us when our hearts have made the connection to each other. You can't explain it, you can't predict it, and you certainly cannot fight it."

"You are most definitely our mate," Mason murmured directly in her ear. "Both man and leopard recognize that you are. The mating bond is now entirely up to you."

"I'm not sure I can do that, not until this is

finished," Violet whispered, and even she could hear the pain in her tone. Mason tensed behind a moment before he moved quickly to swing her into his arms and strode back to the daybed, placing her on his lap while Jacob tugged her legs onto his lap as he sat down beside them.

"By that I assume you mean the fight you're waging against Santiago," Jacob said, watching her intently. "What's the end game for you, baby? If he's dead and gone and the streets are safer, is that finished for you? Because I have a feeling that by cutting off one head of this beast, another will simply rise to take its place. Kieran has long believed that Santiago is only a middle man, that there is someone bigger, badder, and meaner out there, looking at Chicago as a lynchpin in their business plan."

Violet took a deep breath. From her position she could look into both Mason's and Jacob's face at the same time. "The only time in the first twelve years of my life that I felt loved, was when I was with my Poppa. The rest of the time it was about training to be the best, trying to remain invisible to avoid punishment, and staying below the radar. I know what it is like to be threatened and to be so afraid you can't think straight. I will always protect those who need it, that's just who I am."

Violet took a deep breath and shook her head. "Why in the hell am I even telling you this? I don't know you, and I am pretty much ripping the Band-Aid off my past and allowing you both to see the scars."

Mason hugged her tighter, and Jacob rubbed his palm on her leg.

"Perhaps you want us to know the real you," Jacob said gently. "Everything I have seen and am learning about you, baby, tells me what type of person you are, but I think that sometimes you are so far gone on the defensive, you see every action as an attack."

Mason pressed a kiss to her temple. "We do want to get to know you, just as we want to tell you everything about us. It also makes it easier for us to protect you, if we do know everything we can about the people who wish to harm you."

Violet looked between the two men, and for reasons beyond her comprehension she was starting to believe them.

"Baby, you don't have to share everything with us now," Jacob said gently. "We have time. When you are ready you can answer that question you think you've distracted us from."

Violet swallowed the lump that had suddenly appeared in her throat and nodded. A vibration at her wrist had her sitting up and looking at her watch. What she saw was not exactly welcome.

"What is it?" Mason said, his voice little more than a growl. Frowning, Violet looked up at him, her eyes wide in surprise. Both Mason and Jacob's eyes had changed color. There was no sign of the soft metal gray they usually were. Now they were golden amber, and Violet knew she was looking at her leopards.

When did they become mine?

Pushing that thought from her mind she rolled her eyes at them. "Christ, will you guys turn all fur and fang every time my watch vibrates? You had better tell me now, because it's also like a Fitbit and when I reach my step target for the day it might go off unexpectedly. That could be embarrassing for you if we are walking past a dog or something, and you get chased up a tree."

Mason's eyes cleared to gray, and he growled as he leaned in and gently bit down on her shoulder before pulling away. "Smart ass. Enough with the sarcasm, and get to the reason why you looked alarmed."

Violet climbed off him and indicated with her

head for them to follow her. "That was not alarm. That was simple curiosity. Someone has reached out to me."

"Is it Santiago?"

Violet shook her head at Jacob's question. "No, the reaction to that would have been much more extreme and would have been described as fucking amazed, which is a lot closer to alarm than that was. I'd also be trying to find a wooden box big enough for both of you for bringing that fucker to my door. No, it's a woman who works near where you guys came across me last night."

"How do you know that?" Mason asked as she led them back down the iron staircase to her loft, and then behind it to the door that led to her office.

"There are a few people around there that know they can reach out and ask for help, or if they see trouble, and Josie is one of them." Violet walked over to her computers and sat down, typing quickly on the keyboard in front of her and scanned the center screen as it came to life. When the message icon lit up, she clicked on it.

"Umm, hello, this is Josie Cadman." A voice sounded over the speakers, and despite it being a computer connection and a recorded message, Violet could hear the hesitation and concern in young woman's voice. "There is trouble in our neighborhood." The woman gave a nervous giggle. "Again. A group of young guys, all wearing red and white scarves, are running riot. I've seen three muggings in the space of half an hour, and there seems to be a group of them walking into the shopping district. By the way they are carrying pipes, wooden planks, and chains, so I don't think they are coming just to shop. We need help, your kind of help, V. Please."

The recording ended. "Son of a biscuit!"

A low rumble sounded from deep within Mason's

chest. "Diablo's gang wears red and white—" Diablo ran a gang on the west side of the city, and prostitution was one of their main revenue streams, "—and if they have actually sided with Santiago, then his foot soldier numbers just went through the fucking roof."

Violet cursed as she pushed back from her desk. "There goes my quiet afternoon doing my nails." She walked out of the room and headed back towards the lift. When she stepped past the coffee table, she scooped up the bag with the bullet in it. Before she left, she'd set her equipment to run a check on it, and break the chemicals down for her.

Mason pulled his phone from his jeans pocket. "I'll flick a text to our Alpha. I have no doubt that Kieran is mobilizing the pride as we speak, but it would be good for him to know where we're at."

She pressed the button on the lift for the door and stepped in when it opened. She held her palm against the metal panel above the button that would take them to the ground floor. After three seconds it beeped and the lift door closed.

Jacob made an excited sound. "Damn, baby, that is so cool. Biometric?"

Grinning up at him she nodded. "Yep. And now, boys, I would like to show you my lab. You will both need to insert your own mad scientist maniacal evil laughter here as I simply can't do it justice." The door opened, and the three of them stepped out. She sighed happily at everything around her.

"Holy shit," Mason said slowly. "You were right, Jacob. Our mate really is related to Batman."

Violet laughed. "Welcome to my Batcave, boys."

Chapter Six

"You look like shit."

Mason managed a tired laugh at Reggie's astute assessment.

"Wow, Reggie," he said dryly, "you're gonna turn my head if you keep talking to me like that. I mean, what's a guy to think?"

Kieran laughed as he stepped into the foyer just behind him. "I think it's pretty obvious. You do look like shit. Most of us who have been awake for the past thirty-six hours simply *feel* like shit, but you, my friend, have taken it to a whole new level and owned it."

Mason flipped his Alpha off, much to Reggie's obvious amusement. "You have already been cleared from upstairs. The lift is ready and waiting for you." Mason gave him a jaunty salute and walked to the side of the foyer, away from the main bank of lifts as the doors to Violet's personal lift opened. Kieran's raised eyebrows as they stepped in made him smile. "Wait 'til you see the rooftop."

Kieran nodded and stepped into the corner of the lift. "You think your mate knows that I am here with you? I don't want to freak her out, especially if she's as kickass with those fighting batons as you say she is."

The trouble Diablo's men had been intent on causing was not limited to one neighborhood last night, and when reinforcements were needed two neighborhoods to the west of where he, Jacob, and Violet had been, Mason had made the difficult decision to go.

It hadn't been easy, especially for a protective son of a bitch like him, but he had faith that Jacob would watch over Violet, and he knew for a fact that she could take care of herself. When he had left, she had been standing between two young punks using her batons and her sharp sarcasm on both of them indiscriminately. When he'd called out that he needed to go help some of his pridemates who were spread too thin around the city, she had managed to throw him a quick air kiss and a "see you later, kitty cat," before he left.

"Yeah, she knows," Mason replied. "Besides the fact that Jacob is with her and he knows that it was the two of us heading over, she has cameras all over this building. No one gets in or out without her knowledge."

The door swept open into the living area, and Mason took a couple of steps out of the lift and came to a halt. Jacob was sitting on the coffee table grinning like an idiot at him and Kieran, while their mate was fast asleep on the couch in front of the large fire place. She had managed a shower and a change of clothes from the fancy custom fight suit she had been wearing. He and Jacob had watched fascinated as she managed to put a whole arsenal of weaponry into purpose built compartments of that suit. But the yoga pants and oversized t-shirt looked just as amazing on her, and with her hair up in a twist she looked so damn young and innocent his heart ached.

"She fell asleep halfway through a sentence," Jacob said quietly, moving to look back at her, the devotion clear for all to see on his face.

Mason walked closer to look down at her, and he felt his heart clench in his chest. "Is she okay? Was she hurt at all?"

Jacob gave a small laugh. "A couple of bruises, but nothing serious. When she was swinging those damn batons no one could get near her. There were a couple of times when there seemed to be waves of the fuckers coming out of the woodwork and going straight for her—" Mason frowned, not liking the sound of that at all, "—but then she has these tiny metal things that she placed on people that administer an electric shock. They weren't big enough to house enough energy to knock a person unconscious, but enough to distract them enough that she could get close enough to knock them unconscious anyway."

Mason's frown evaporated, and he grinned, loving the sound of that and the fact their mate was so damn kickass. It really was a turn-on.

"Does she know I was coming?" Kieran asked from the entrance. He hadn't taken another step into the apartment, obviously wanting to make sure he was invited. When Jacob nodded Kieran walked further into the room, and sat on the armchair furthest from them, obviously giving her space.

"How long has she been asleep?" Mason asked.

"Not nearly long enough," Violet grumbled sleepily from the couch as she pushed to sit up, sweeping her hair from her face, and blinking sleepily. "Boy, I thought cats were quiet. You two are terrible."

Jacob laughed. "Yeah, Mason and Kieran can be a little on the rowdy side."

Violet turned to level Jacob with a look. "I was talking about you and Mason." She turned to look over at Kieran, who was staring openly at her, and Mason saw her eyes lighten in color. "That one's silent."

Mason looked between his mate and his Alpha as they stared at each other in wary silence. "Okay, well, Violet, this is our Alpha, Kieran Murphy. Alpha this is our mate, Violet Riccitelli."

Violet stared at their Alpha for a moment then blinked a couple of times before relaxing back on the couch.

"So, do I pass inspection, Ms. Violet?" Kieran asked dryly.

Violet grinned. "For now. I can only read auras. I

can't see the past or the future, and I certainly cannot read your mind, but the colors I see in your aura tell me a little about you. Your aura, although not perfect, rings with loyalty, honor, and a strong sense of what is right. Your mama lion raised you right! So, yep, for now you do pass inspection. Until you do something monumentally stupid and I have to beat some sense into you."

Kieran threw back his head and laughed. "Damn, you are more than a match for these two. I kinda wish I met you first. I might have given them a run for their money."

Twin growls erupted into the apartment, and Jacob rose slowly from the coffee table to stand shoulder to shoulder with Mason. In unison they turned and both glared at their Alpha. Kieran's eyes turned amber, and Mason could feel the pressure of the man's dominance filling the room. He and Jacob both withstood the pressure for as long as they could, but within seconds they fell beneath it and knelt on one knee on the floor. Their Alpha was dominant and strong as fuck, but it had been a while since Mason had felt it used against him though.

"It would be best for you, if you let them up now, Alpha kitty." Violet's voice was cold, her tone deadly, not one he had heard her use before, and Mason's growl of displeasure immediately shut off as he stared over at his mate in concern. She had moved to stand up beside the couch, and there was a gun in her hand. He had no idea where she had grabbed it from.

"Violet." His words were slightly garbled because his canines had descended, but he heard the desperation in his tone. "It's okay, Jacob and I challenged him."

"We did, baby," Jacob confirmed in a clear voice, obviously not having to battle with his leopard like

Mason was. "He was just reminding us of the order of things."

Violet nodded. "Oh, I know how it goes. I've watched *Animal Planet*. I get how the head lion has to fight off the other lions for the right to mount the lionesses, but that it is not going to happen! I am just not that into you, Alpha kitty."

The pressure dissolved immediately, allowing him and Jacob to get to their feet, and when Mason looked over at Kieran, he was shocked to see his Alpha's cheeks with a sweep of red across them.

"What, no! Wait, I—you," Kieran stuttered, and Mason couldn't hide his grin. He had never seen his Alpha flustered before. "Sorry, let me try that again. Violet, I have no wish to *mount* you."

Violet's brow rose. "And why the hell not? I happen to know I am extremely mountable. You should *be* so lucky to get a piece of this." She ran a hand down her side. "What, you think you can do better than me?'

"Not at all!" Kieran held up his hands in a supplicating manner. "You're hot! Honestly, if you were single and not mated to two of my pride I would be all over you. But this is—" Violet made a small sound, and Kieran's eyes narrowed. "Son of a bitch, you're fucking with me, aren't you?"

Violet grinned as she lowered the gun her side. "Maybe just a little. Sorry, when you get to know me you'll learn that I am fluent in sarcasm, and according to my ever patient assistant, smart ass is my second language."

Kieran nodded. "So noted. I will be sure to run everything you say through my internal bullshit-o-meter from now on."

"That would probably be a good idea." Violet winked in his direction and reengaged the safety on her weapon. Mason knew she did that deliberately. She hadn't pulled that gun for show. Her words may have had a playful tone, but her intent to shoot was absolutely there. If Kieran had reacted differently, she had been prepared to use the weapon.

"And that is noted as well," Kieran said dryly as he relaxed back in the armchair. "I wanted to thank you for agreeing to have a look at that bullet." Kieran's face fell slightly, and Mason knew he was thinking about Jason.

"I've analyzed the chemical compounds on the bullet."

Mason turned to look at his mate with shock. *When the hell did she find time to do that?*

"There were traces of a neuromuscular block and an anticoagulant. The first one is designed to create paralysis and is often used as an anesthetic. The second stops your blood from clotting. The effect of those would have worn off eventually."

"Could either of those force a shift?"

Violet thought about that for a moment then nodded. "I believe it would. From what I have read, your animals are a part of you, and your musculoskeletal system changes within you. The change is very quick, and I would think painful, but then your feline genes would come into their own and the change would be completed." That had to be the most clinical description Mason had ever heard about a shift, but it sounded right. "A neuromuscular block would create a type of paralysis in the musculoskeletal system, and I'm pretty sure that would force the change."

Kieran nodded, amber flickering in his eyes. "And the anticoagulant means that our blood won't clot. Without the wounds clotting, there is no way for our healing abilities to take hold and heal the wound.

Fucking bastard."

Violet nodded. "Yep, Santiago is a bastard, and one that deserves to die a horrible death somewhere I can watch with a bowl of popcorn and a beer. But what he's got on those bullets, we can counter."

Kieran nodded, and he relaxed back into his chair. "Thank you. Without something to fight the effects of those fucking bullets, I've had to tell my team to keep their animals in check. So, tell me, Violet, what did Santiago do that put him on your shit list?"

Violet sat back down on the couch, and tucked her legs up under her. "You want just one reason? I would have thought you'd know of at least a dozen reasons why that asshole would end up on a person's shit list."

"I do, most definitely, but what I am wondering is why a woman like yourself, with the obvious resources that you have, would bother. We now know that you have sponsored trusts and programs for the families of his victims. You have purchased stocks, offices, and store fronts for businesses he has screwed over. So what's with all the Good Samaritan shit?"

"And I can't just be a Good Samaritan?" Violet asked with an exaggerated flutter of her eyelashes. Mason was starting to get a very good read on his mate. She used her sarcasm and her humor as an effective diversion when a conversation was stepping into areas she wasn't keen on going.

"Of course you can, and I have no doubt that you are," Mason said as he sat down on the couch next to his mate, Jacob taking her other side. "But I think that there might be more to it than that. When we asked you a couple of days ago if he knew who you were, you side stepped the question. I think there was more to the story than you let on."

Violet was silent for a moment, looking down at where her fingers were playing with an imaginary piece of lint on her shirt.

"Violet," Kieran began as he leaned forward in his chair. "I know that we are on the same team, and I hope like hell you can figure out how to counter Santiago's fucking bullets and you will fight with us. Not just to help me protect my pride, but because this fucker is taking women from the streets and from their families and selling them into the sex trade. I cannot allow that to happen in my city. I would also love to know why I get the feeling that you feel guilty about the crimes committed by Roberto Santiago."

Violet's gaze flew to his Alpha, and Mason knew he had it right. "Because I do, Alpha Kitty. How could I not? I had the opportunity to end that man twelve years ago, and I failed."

****

Violet felt a pressure building with her chest. It was as if someone had placed a weight directly on her, and it was restricting her breathing. In a slight panic, she pushed up off the couch and stepped around the coffee table to pace a little.

"Every single person that man has sold into slavery, or had killed, or the lives he has ruined in the past twelve years, is because I failed," Violet confessed. "This morning, I caught up with Josie Cadman, to thank her for alerting us to Diablo's gang mobilizing for Santiago. He is directly responsible for the deaths of her parents, and the disappearance of her sister, leaving her all alone in the world. How do you think it feels to stand there talking to her, knowing that it was a man I had failed to kill that took her loved ones from her? I had him, dead to rights."

Mason leaned forward in the couch, placing his

elbows on his knees. "Violet, you're what, twenty-two years old?"

"Twenty-four, but to be fair, some of those years counted for at least, like seven years because of how much they sucked."

Mason smiled at her. "Well, even at twenty-four years old that means that you were only twelve at the time. You should never have been placed in the position to have or want to kill a man at that age, let alone take on the burden of guilt for having not done it. No matter who that man is."

"And if that man is my father?" Violet swallowed hard. Saying it out loud after all these years had seemed almost impossible until she'd actually done it. She looked around at the three men in the room expecting to see horror, or disgust on their faces, but there was nothing but acceptance.

And more confusingly from Mason and Jacob, a healthy amount of pride as well.

"We wondered if you'd find the courage to tell us, baby," Jacob said gently, and Violet sat down hard on the ottoman beside her.

"You knew?" Her voice was little more than a whisper. "How did you know? I have done everything in my power to keep that hidden. Not to mention Santiago himself went to great lengths to ensure that any reference of a daughter was removed and lost forever. How could you possibly know?"

"You know better than to expect that by simply deleting something on the internet would mean it was gone forever," Kieran answered. "Despite the atrocities your father is responsible for, you do come from a great man. Stefano Riccitelli was an honorable man. Someone I am very proud to have met."

Violet wrapped her arms around her midriff,

suddenly feeling chilled. "You knew my Poppa?"

Kieran nodded his expression sad. "Mostly he knew my dad, but yeah, I did, too. He was a friend to the Black Ridge pride when my dad was Alpha. You and I met once when you were with him and he visited. You could have only been about six or seven, and your hair was black then. Your Poppa was livid because you'd come to him for a visit and were covered in cuts and bruises. I remember my dad telling him they were consistent with fighting, but not the type of schoolyard fights one might have suspected a child of that age engaging in. These were way more intense."

Violet searched her memory, and vaguely remembered a time when she had been with her Poppa and visiting some "friends". The memory was more vivid than most, because Poppa had been so angry. Not at her, never at her, but definitely at her father, not that he gave a shit. During the visit, she did remember a dark haired little boy, older than her by a few years, but still a boy. He had played with her for a while, just some innocuous board game, but it distracted her from the adult conversations around her.

"You played a board game with me," Violet nodded as the memory cleared. "I won, from memory."

Kieran grinned. "Yeah, but I totally let you." His expression turned somber. "I was distracting you from the conversation because Stefano was there to ask my dad to help him remove your father from the equation. He could no longer stand by and allow what Santiago was getting involved in, to touch his beloved granddaughter, but Santiago had gotten too damn powerful, and he couldn't take you out of that environment without help." Kieran looked away for a moment, before leveling his stare at her. "But my dad said no. He looked over at you, and despite how withdrawn you were, and the bruises you had on you, he said every little girl deserves to have a father."

Violet wanted to scream a denial at that. Roberto had never been a father to her, not really. And to have that be the reason for the head of this pride not taking steps or measures against the man laying siege to this city, was an insult. Something in her expression must have given the men an insight into what she was thinking.

"Violet, my dad was a great man, but he made mistakes, too, and in this case he made a huge one. If you think that the fault of your father and everything he has done in the past dozen years should be placed at your feet, then our pride is just as guilty for the actions that he has committed since that day."

In that moment Violet realized that perhaps the blame was never hers to bear and it should sit firmly with the man who had been responsible.

"There's certainly someone else who should take the blame for what happened in the last two days," Mason snarled, and Violet turned to see a look of distain on his face. "Whoever this fucking IEH organization is, they need to take some of the responsibility for the blood spilled in Chicago."

Violet frowned. "Why would you say that? Everything I have read from this organization has been nothing but truth. They tell the people that there is a war going on right under their noses, and that they need to take notice and be part of the solution."

"But they also invite retaliation," Jacob argued. "Think about it, baby. Do you think there would have been as much bloodshed and pain caused in the past two days if they hadn't sent that last message? It cannot be a coincidence that everything started less than a day after it was released."

Violet shook her head. "I don't accept that. The last message called for the city to stop turning their backs on what is happening right in front of them. There was nothing in there that identified some of the shit Santiago is up to, or the crimes that he is guilty of. It was a call to action for everyone who calls Chicago home to stand up and take notice of what is happening in their neighborhood, and when they see an injustice, or they witness a crime, they do something about it. I did not see anything in that communication that could have sparked the violence of the last two days."

"The last part of that message said that *Santiago* had to be stopped," Marcel pointed out. "It called out his name, and said he needed to be stopped by any means and at all costs. How could he not see that as a threat?"

"You know," Kieran's voice held a tone Violet did not care for, and when she turned toward him, his eyes had a distinct amber hue to them, "you are starting to sound a little like this IEH organization yourself."

Violet narrowed her gaze at the lion, and despite noticing the air pressure change in the room, a clear sign that his dominance was leaving an impression in the room, she remained unaffected. "That makes perfect sense. IEH stands for the Latin *Iustitia et Hyacinthinum.*" Mason made a sound at that last word, no doubt recognizing it. "You will not find that anywhere, and there is no formal listing of that name in full. As far as the American Government and the city of Chicago are concerned the name of the business is IEH. But it stands for *Iustitia et Hyacinthinum,* and means Justice for Violet. I wrote that message. I am IEH."

Chapter Seven

"Well, that went well," Mason said dryly, and Jacob fought the urge to reach out and punch him.

"If by going well you mean fucking horrendously bad, then yep, it did." Jacob cursed under his breath and looked over at the door their mate had exited through moments before. After her announcement that she was in fact IEH, all three of the shifters had laid into her. Mostly out of concern for her, but that was not how their Violet had taken it. Santiago may not know who she was, but by deliberately antagonizing him she was putting a large as fuck target on her head.

Kieran had said she was playing a dangerous game, and may have mentioned something about foolish actions, and their mate had seen red and kicked him out. Kieran had left immediately, but from the continuous growl that rumbled through his chest, Jacob knew he didn't liked what he had heard any more than Mason and Jacob had. After he had left, and they had calmed down a little more, she went on to add that she was also taking business and contracts out from beneath Santiago, and their fear rose to epic proportions.

They had yelled at her a second time, effectively forcing both feet into their mouths simultaneously as far as she was concerned. In what Jacob was starting to see as typical of how Violet dealt with upsetting situations, she attacked verbally, not giving them a chance to talk, and stormed out of the room. They had hurt her and she was pissed, and he kind of couldn't blame her.

"Do you think she'll ever calm down enough to let us in that door?"

"God, I hope so." Mason stood up and moved to the door she had walked through. Just as he raised his hand to knock, they picked up the sound of her voice from behind the door.

"I really think I should just shoot them both, Dot," Violet said, and he and Mason shared a confused look. No one had gone into the room with her, so who the hell was Dot?

"Well, you could do that." A woman's voice that echoed and sounded slightly off and Jacob knew she was talking to someone via a computer. "But I don't think you should. It sounds to me that they are worried about you, V. And that is something that I applaud, and not something that I would sentence two men to death for. Besides, didn't we already determine that they are hot?"

Violet harrumphed but didn't deny it, and Jacob wanted to roar in pleasure. Their mate thought they were hot, so things were looking up!

"Just because they are easy on the eyes doesn't mean they can go spouting stupid stuff to a grown ass woman," Violet groused, then a moment later groaned. "But the thing is, Dot, they are right. Them and Alpha Kitty called it correctly. That message enraged Santiago to the point he aligned with Diablo's gang and he sent his men out to make a point."

"So if they're right, why are you getting all shitty?"

Jacob vowed to buy that woman flowers just as soon as he found out who she was and where she lived.

"Because I hate it when someone else points out my mistakes, you know that." Violet sounded tired.

"Violet, my sweet, you do what you do because you are trying to make the world a better place. I know that, and I would hazard a guess that those two shifters know that, too. But you take too many risks, and I for one am afraid for you when you do go toe to toe with that bastard."

Violet mumbled, and Jacob thought she might

have said, "I know how to take care of myself."

Dot laughed. "I know you do, V. But sometimes, the best part of life and having relationships with people that care about you, is knowing that they would do everything in their power to take care of you. Just as I know you take care of me and my Johnny, and I'm pretty sure you would do the same for those leopards of yours."

Jacob liked the sound of that. Being called hers was definitely something he could get used to.

"How is it going anyway?" Violet asked, but Jacob knew she would be processing the advice her friend gave her.

"It is going really well! You got the contract, and the ministry was so pleased they've waived the probation period and want you committed to the fix as soon as possible. Johnny and I crossed the strait over to the South Island yesterday and plan to do a wine tour this afternoon."

He had no guilt about eavesdropping on the first half of that conversation, but Jacob felt a little bad listening to this part, so he tapped Mason's arm and the two of the moved off into the kitchen.

"Well that was … interesting," Mason said with a huge grin on his face, and Jacob had to agree with him. They had learned more about their mate, and how her feelings were starting to grow for him and Mason, and they would forever be indebted to Dot.

Mason walked into the large gourmet kitchen, stood with his hands on his hips, and completed a three hundred and sixty degree turn.

"What are you doing?" Jacob had to ask, taking a seat on one of the barstools at the kitchen island.

"I'm starving," Mason admitted as he started opening cupboards in the kitchen. "I've been dealing to those fuckers for two days straight, shifting between my animal form and human form repeatedly, and I need food."

"Cool, whatever you're cooking make it a double. I could definitely eat."

Mason stopped his random spinning and looked around helplessly. "Sure, but if it's not edible, then don't blame me. Christ, have you ever seen a more complicated kitchen? All I want to do is find the fridge, grab some eggs, a skillet, and cook us some scrambled eggs, but I recognize nothing in this kitchen."

A soft click sounded in the room, signaling a door opening, and Jacob swung around on his chair to face the door his mate had just walked out of.

Is she going to throw us out, too?

She walked into the kitchen, refusing to meet his or Mason's eye. "Firstly, you should never put eggs in the fridge." Obviously she had been listening to their conversation somehow, but he figured calling her on it would be a little pot, kettle, black so stayed quiet. "If you do, they lose their flavor. And although the eggs I keep in the pantry are tasty, not adding tomatoes, prosciutto, parmesan, and capsicum is almost criminal."

Neither he nor Mason moved, not sure what to do, and simply watched as their mate moved with confidence around her kitchen. She opened panels that he had thought were simply wall panels to reveal a walk in pantry, and pulled out a skillet from a cupboard under the stovetop.

"You might have noticed something about me," Violet said quietly, still not turning to look them in the eye. "I tend to fly off the handle every now and then and overreact. It's not something I am proud of, and I am sorry for yelling at you."

"I think we were the first to do that yelling, Violet," Mason said. "Perhaps if we all make an effort not to yell too much and let the other person talk, we might avoid an argument or two."

Violet shot them a glance and a small smile. "Agreed. And I will try. I'm sure to slip up at least a lot, but I will definitely try."

"Can we help, baby?" Jacob asked quietly and smiled gently when she looked up and met his gaze.

"Can you crack an egg into a bowl without adding shell?" Her tone was shy, but there was a thread of humor.

"Nope," he deadpanned, and she giggled.

She turned to Mason and raised a brow in question, and his brother shook his head with a grin. "Sorry, little one, our mother banned us from the kitchen at a young age. The only help you will get from us is fetching stuff from the pantry and doing the dishes. Anything else and you are taking your life into your own hands in all honesty."

Violet laughed. "Thanks for the warning. Why don't you head into my room and grab a quick shower while I get some dinner going?" Mason thanked her with a quick kiss, and Jacob watched as a sweep of color graced her beautiful face.

Without skipping a beat, Violet went back to chopping the ingredients, cracking the eggs, and whisking them together with a confidence that spoke of considerable skill. In what seemed like no time at all, she had toast on, omelets cooking, and the kitchen filling with the most delicious smells. Jacob entertained her with stories from his childhood and embellished a few when they made her laugh.

By the time Mason returned, they were ready to eat. The three of them sat down at the table, the lights of the city around them twinkling through the windows, and their conversation remained light and easy. Jacob was hard pressed to remember when he'd last enjoyed an evening as much as he was enjoying this one.

When she stood and reached out to start clearing the table, Jacob grabbed her hand. "Like we said before, baby, Mason and I are worthless in the cooking department, but I can wash a dish within an inch of its life."

"And the way I use a towel should be outlawed," Mason added with a grin. The two of them took care of tidying up while their mate chatted with them from her place at the kitchen island sipping a cup of coffee. After a while, her conversation died away, and she stared into the bottom of her cup. Jacob finished up and turned to lean against the sink, drying his hands on a towel as he watched her carefully.

"So, will you get in trouble because I threw Kieran out?" Violet asked after a while, not taking her gaze from the cup in her hand. Jacob wondered if she knew she had referred to him by name rather than the nickname she had given him.

Mason shook his head as he placed the tea towel on the bench. "Not at all. Kieran has already texted me to tell you he apologizes for upsetting you, and hopes you know that his anger was born out of concern for you. The guilt you feel about Santiago is one shared by Kieran and now the entire Black Ridge pride, and he wants to be sure you know that you have more than just allies in this city, you have family."

Violet jolted back in shock. "Family? He said that?"

"Yeah, he did because it's true," Jacob said with a shrug, "and not just because you are the mate for two of his pride, but because of the fight you fight and the values you live by. They resonate with us as a pride. Family and connections are the most important things in the world to us, and it means we take care of each other. There is no greater importance than pride."

Violet stared at them, and Jacob thought she looked a little pale. "And he sees me as part of the family?" she whispered.

Jacob pushed off from the bench and moved around the kitchen island to stand beside his mate. Whether it was the growing connection between them or his own imagination he couldn't tell, but he felt he could sense her emotions getting the best of her. "He sees you as a member of our pride. You will always have Mason and me protecting you, and if anything happens to us, then the pride will be there for you."

Mason, who had stepped up behind their mate, wrapped an arm around her shoulder. "Always, little one. You're not alone anymore."

Chapter Eight

You're not alone anymore.

The words sounded alien to her, but they repeated over and over in her mind. She had been alone from the moment her Poppa had died. For the past twelve years she had worked with a single-minded focus. Make as much money as possible, train as hard as she could, and destroy anything and everything Santiago touched. Up until that moment she had not realized that she had never taken the time to grieve. She had been alone. So very alone.

She opened her mouth to say something, what it was she had no idea, but no words came out. Just a single brokenhearted sob, and then as if that were the dam that held back all her tears, all her pain rose to the top and consumed her. She gave herself over to her tears, and cried. She cried for her Poppa and for every one of the people Santiago had killed or destroyed from the moment she failed to kill him. She cried for the childhood that she had been robbed of, and the future she had embraced in the name of vengeance. And by the time she'd finished she felt completely empty.

When she finally managed to open eyes that felt extremely gritty, she found herself on her bed, pressed between Mason and Jacob. She had no recollection of having been carried into the bedroom. The bedside light was on low and cast a warm light around her room, and she took comfort in her familiar surroundings as she quieted. She lay completely relaxed, held tight to Mason's chest with Jacob pressed from shoulder to knee behind her. Neither of them had said anything. They'd simply held her as the storm had consumed her, and now that it had ended, she felt almost cleansed.

"You okay, love?" Mason asked and she felt the

rumble of his words against her.

She sniffed and nodded. "Sorry about that." Her voice was husky, and if she wasn't mistaken there was a touch of relief there, too.

"No need to apologize," Mason said gently as he pressed a kiss to her temple. "I have a feeling that was a long time coming."

Unable to think of what to say, Violet simply nodded and snuggled a little deeper into their embrace. She froze at the feel of the hard evidence of both men's arousal against her.

"Um, well, I—ah." Violet cringed at her rambling, never having ever been in a situation where her verbal skills abandoned her. Both men chuckled.

"It's fine, little one." Mason laughed as he pressed another kiss to her temple. "There is no way in the world we could control our reaction to finally having you in our arms and between us. Just ignore it."

Violet huffed a laugh. "You've got to be kidding right? Saying ignore you is like saying don't bother eating the salted caramel butter cream from your cupcake because the plain vanilla cake underneath it is much nicer."

"I don't know if I like being compared to a cupcake icing," Jacob said dryly from behind her, and she giggled.

"Well, that depends. I am the lick the icing off first kinda girl," Violet said innocently.

Both men were quiet for a moment, and then twin growls filled the air. "You're playing with fire, little one," Mason groaned as his lips went to her neck, placing nibbling kisses along her jawline. Violet moaned at the sensation, arching back into Jacob to feel the strength of him behind her, and was enjoying the slow burn of arousal building with her with Mason tensed against her.

"Damn it," he snarled. "You've just cried your heart out and are probably emotionally drained by everything you've heard today. Jacob and I are not going to take advantage of you like that."

Jacob groaned. "Despite how damn good it feels."

"How about I take advantage of the two of you?" Violet countered. "Would that be okay?" She reached out and pressed kisses against Mason's jaw, loving the feel of the light stubble against her lips.

Mason groaned, arching his neck to give her better access, a move she made the most of. "Yeah, I think we would be okay with that."

Jacob chuckled as he gently rolled his hips against her. "Just for the record, Mason and I would have both stood down, and simply held you while you slept. It would have been painful as hell, but we would have done it with smiles on our faces. Now, oh baby, now we get to show you what it is like to be loved on by two shifters who adore you."

Jacob slid down the bed to kneel by her knees, and helped her to lay the bottom half of her body flat against the mattress. His hands went to the waistband of the yoga pants she wore, and she lifted up as he slid her pants and panties off in one move, leaving her lying naked from the waist down on her bed.

"Holy Mary mother of all things hotter than hot," Jacob whispered and she groaned when his hands slid down over her abdomen. "Look at you, Violet. So hot, so sexy, so fucking bare."

Mason sat up to look down her body, and he groaned before looking down at her. She could see the amber of his leopard in his gaze, battling with the arousal that hovered there. Her mind whirled at how fast things were moving, but was stopped in its tracks when Mason leaned down and slammed his mouth against hers.

Vaguely she was aware as Jacob gently urged her to part her legs, but the movement was lost on her as she gave herself over to Mason's mouth. His kiss was all consuming, and she felt as if she were drowning in his flavor and his heat when she felt Jacob lick between her thighs.

She cried out, but the sound was caught by Mason's mouth.

"Damn, baby, you are delicious." Jacob's voice was deeper than usual, and she wondered for a moment if Jacob's leopard was just as close to the surface as Mason's, but then Jacob placed his mouth on her again and all thought fled beneath the maelstrom of pleasure that cascaded over her.

Jacob made small circles around her clit with his tongue, and Violet shivered then screamed when he sucked her into his mouth, flicking her tongue against her in a fast rhythm. Violet had not been with many men— hell, there had only been that one guy in college, and the experience had not exactly left her with great memories. She had pleasured herself in the past. What woman hadn't? But for her to reach climax, it was a long hard road to get her to that level of excitement, but apparently, when it came to Jacob and Mason Williams, that wasn't so much the case.

An orgasm slammed through her unexpectedly and had her pulling away from Mason's kiss and arching off the bed with a scream. The intensity of her release had her reaching down to grasp Jacob's head in her hands and rolling her hips to meet the frantic movements of his mouth, and the waves of her release rolled on and on as every muscle within her seemed to tense. When her pleasure began to ebb, she slumped back to the mattress, desperately trying to draw enough oxygen into her lungs.

As the blood stopped roaring in her ears, she heard Jacob's constant growl, and loved the way he continued to work his mouth between her legs, taking everything she had to offer, and loving on her through the most explosive release of her life. When she quieted, Jacob pressed one last kiss against her then moved up her body, until he was straddling her hips. She looked up into his face, and felt her heart turn over at the emotions written for all to see in his expression.

He was pleased, and the satisfaction he felt was evident in his grin, but it was the emotion swirling within his eyes that had her biting her lip. She was too afraid to put a name to that emotion in that moment, but she had a good idea what it was.

"Come up here, baby," Jacob said and helped her to sit up. "Let's get you comfortable." He pulled her shirt up and over her head, and she knew in that moment she was more than a little shell-shocked because she allowed him to bare her torso. She hadn't bothered with a bra when she'd climbed out of the shower so when the shirt slipped over her head she was naked.

Both men inhaled sharply, and Violet's hands flew to the scar on her chest. It was an ugly array of scar tissue and puckered skin, and they would have known from the sheer size of it that it had to have been a critical wound, especially being near the heart as that was.

"Baby?" Jacob whispered the question, but Violet shook her head. She wasn't quite ready to share that story yet, and she kept her gaze on Jacob's abdominals, refusing to lift her gaze any higher.

Jacob gently placed his hands on hers and tugged until she drew her hands away, leaving her scar completely visible.

"You have nothing to hide, baby. You are so damn beautiful you make my heart ache." Jacob whispered as he gently leaned in and pressed kisses against the scar tissue, telling her with his touch and his actions that the scar didn't faze him.

When he pulled up and leaned in to kiss her, Violet moved to meet him. Jacob's kiss was softer and slower than Mason's had been moments before, but no less intense, and she shivered beneath the power of his kiss.

When he pulled back, Violet's hair tumbled free of the clip she'd pulled it up with, and fell in a riot of red curls down her back. "That's better. I have a lot of fantasies in my mind that feature your hair."

Just as she was about to ask what they were, Jacob slid to the side and then Mason was beside her. She had a glimpse of toned and muscled male flesh for a brief moment, before she was lifted and encouraged to straddle his thighs. She sat back a little on his thighs trapping Mason's erection beneath her.

"Fuck," Mason muttered as he closed his eyes for a moment. "The feel of all your soft beautiful skin on mine is addictive. I want you. I want to feel you take my cock as far into you as I can get, and I want to watch as you shatter around me. But right now, baby, if I lead I am going to fuck you too hard, and I am so damn scared of hurting you." He urged her to kneel up over him, until the head of his cock nestled against the sensitive opening of her pussy. "This way you lead the charge. You take control of the speed and intensity."

Violet swallowed a sudden lump that had formed in her throat. Since meeting Mason and Jacob she had done a little research on her own, and she'd learned that leopards were very much a dominant shifter race. They very rarely like to give up control, and it meant a lot to her that Mason would hand her the reins for their first time.

Rotating her hips gently, she slid down on him, sliding the head of his cock into her pussy inch by inch. She took her time, not because she was in any kind of discomfort despite his girth, but because of the intense look on Mason's face. His gaze was locked to where their bodies were joined and his body tensed beneath her.

"Jesus," he whispered reverently, and she watched as color rose into his cheeks. "That has to be the hottest damn thing I have ever seen in my life. The way your body shifts and molds itself to take mine, is so fucking humbling."

With one last revolution of her hips, Violet sighed when she was finally nestled on his thighs and Mason's cock was buried deep within her. "Wow, that feels good. So full and hot." Violet barely recognized her own voice.

"The view from here is pretty fucking spectacular, too." Jacob's voice was more a growl, and he was lying with his head on his hands beside them, simply staring up at her with intense amber eyes.

Mason ran his hands down her back until he cupped her ass. "Move on me, little one. Ride me, take me the way you want to, fuck me and make me yours."

Violet's smile was wicked. "You bet your sweet ass I will, kitty cat. Now, hold on tight. I like to ride hard." Mason's answering laugh morphed into a grin as Violet lifted up then slammed back down, adding a rotation of her hips when she bottomed out, driving her clit against the hard muscles of his abdomen.

"Fuck!" Mason groaned, his fingers clenching convulsively on her hips.

Violet gripped his shoulders hard, leaning back a little, and began to move. She lifted and fell in a steady rhythm, taking him at his word, and riding him the way she wanted to. She kept her eyes on him, watching as amber bled into the grey and she knew his leopard was close to the surface.

"There's my leopard," she whispered, and his eyes blazed with heat. She opened her psychic sense and watched as his aura appeared before her. Where Mason's aura was part cat, part man, when his leopard was this close to the surface, he was more feline than anything else. His aura rang with dominance and possession, and a loyalty and devotion that took her breath away.

Blinking hard she concentrated on taking him hard and fast. She could feel her body tightening and knew that her orgasm was thundering toward her at frightening speed, and she refused to succumb to it without ensuring Mason achieved his release at the same time.

She moved faster, driving her hips up and down in a hard and fast rhythm. She added a gyration each time she settled on his thigh knowing that it pleased him as much as it did her. She gritted her teeth and clamped down tight on him when her orgasm seemed inevitable and she reveled in Mason's shout. His body tensed beneath her, and as she screamed her release to the room, she felt him shudder beneath her, and his cock swell within her. She could feel the heat of his release in every fiber of her being.

Gasping for air, she fell forward, her hips circling tightly, ensuring that she milked as much out of her orgasm as well as his. They both shuddered when her clit pressed against him and a ripple of sensation fluttered through her pussy, no doubt undulating against him where he was still buried to the hilt within her.

When the sparks of pleasure that had been rolling through her ebbed away, she collapsed completely against him, sighing when his arms reached up to wrap around her waist and hold her tighter to him.

"Jesus, Violet—" Mason said breathlessly. "That

was the most powerful thing I have ever felt in my life. You slay me, little one."

Violet hugged him tighter and buried her nose in his neck, inhaling his scent before pulling back to meet his gaze. "For me, too." Her voice was a little hoarse, no doubt from all the screaming she had been doing.

Mason smiled as he reached up to gently sweep her hair from her face. "As much as I want to hold you in my arms and cuddle you for at least the next thirty to fifty years—" Violet smiled at that, but it didn't stop a kernel of joy from blooming within her chest, "—I think there's someone here who is need of a little of your attention, too."

"Too fucking right I am," Jacob growled from beside them. "The hottest thing in the world is watching you shatter like that, baby, and more than my next breath I want to feel you shatter again, but this time while you are wrapped around my cock. But if you are too sore, or tired, then I can wait."

The painful look on his face told Violet that although he would wait, it would take its toll. Amazingly, despite the intense release she had just experienced, arousal began to thread its way through her body. Kneeling up, she sighed at the feel of Mason's cock slipping from inside her, and moved to the side of the bed.

"Oh, I think I can find the energy to go a round with you. Jacob," Violet's voice was almost a purr, and from the way Jacob's eyes turned amber she knew he liked the sound of it. She crawled toward him, then up and over his chest so she could capture his mouth with her own.

He led her lead for a few moments, and she reveled in the freedom of it. She swept her tongue into his mouth and moaned at the exotic flavor of him. When she sucked his lip into her mouth and pressed her teeth into the flesh, he groaned, and she knew his control and patience snapped.

Jacob's hands reached up into her hair, gripping it in his hands, and Violet moaned when he tugged her head to the angle he wanted, then attacked her mouth. She moaned as he licked and bit into her mouth, claiming her mouth as his own as surely as Mason had. She gasped with shock when she felt a wet warmth between her legs and she pulled back from his kiss.

"Just cleaning you up, little one," Mason said with a grin, continuing to wipe a warm facecloth between her legs and her face bloomed with color.

"I could have done that."

Mason shook his head. "Hell no! That is most definitely our job and our privilege."

She would have argued more, but Jacob turned her head back to him gently and took her mouth with his a second time, rolling so that he was lying completely over her, and she wrapped her legs around his hips. The hot, hard feel of his erection pressed against her abdomen had her pussy releasing more hot liquid.

"Damn," Jacob moaned as he moved his lips down her neck to her breast, flicking her nipple with his tongue. "I can smell you arousal in the air, and it is the sweetest damn temptation in the world. I want to spend some time with my mouth on your pussy in the worst way—" Violet moaned, and her pussy clenched at the thought, "but I am beyond the level of control I would need to do that without coming on your bedspread like an untrained teenager." Jacob lifted his head and grinned up at her. "Rain check?"

Violet giggled. "Well, if I am going to have to take a rain check for that, I'll want you to get your mouth on me, while I have both your cocks at my disposal."

"Deal!" Both her men said at the same time, and she laughed. She would never have thought that sex could be fun, and that laughter would be just as important as the intense moments, but for the three of them, it was.

Jacob knelt up and shuffled off the end of the bed onto his feet, grabbing her by the hips and tugging her so that her ass now sat on the edge of the bed. "I'm glad we have the second act of our first night together sorted. But for now, I really do need to fuck you."

Violet grinned as she ran her hands up and over her breasts, reveling in Jacob's guttural groan. She watched as he suddenly reached down to grip the base of his cock, and his expression turned intense.

"Goddamn it!" Jacob cursed. "You are just too damn sexy for my own good. I was all set to fuck you like this, taking you good and deep and watching your expression as you came, but if I have to watch you fucking touch yourself, this will be over way to soon."

Violet squeaked a shocked sound when Jacob suddenly flipped her onto her stomach with ease, and she was bent over the end of the bed, her feet barely touching the floor due to the extra height of the bed she'd had made to make the most of the view when she lay down at night.

She groaned when she felt Jacob's cock press against her and he buried himself deep within her with one solid thrust. She loved the bed even more now that it meant Jacob and Mason could take her this way. She felt full, and when Jacob pulled out then thrust back in, she cried out as he moved over something within her that had her jolting with pleasure.

"Oh, yeah," Mason said from his spot sitting up on the bed, leaning against the headboard. "Jacob's hitting your sweet spot in that position, isn't he?"

Violet had no idea what that meant, but when

Jacob moved again she cried out. Jacob growled deep, and she felt the mattress move as his fists landed on either side of her hips.

"This is going to go quick, baby," Jacob panted. "I'll make it up to you next time."

Violet wanted to say he was doing just fine this time, but lost the ability to think let alone speak when Jacob began to pound into her. She reached out and gripped the bedclothes, her toes curling into the carpet as she had to just lie there and take what he had to give. And oh, how she loved the way he gave it.

She jerked up and off the mattress when her orgasm struck without warning, and she screamed Jacob's name to the world at large. Over her own screams, she heard Jacob roar her name in response and reveled in the jolts of his hips against her as he came. Violet sobbed her pleasure into the mattress. Everything would be different now. Being with Jacob and Mason like this had her shattering into a million tiny little pieces, and she had no idea how she would ever be able to pull herself back together again, if it didn't work out between them.

Chapter Nine

"I think he's dead," Vincenzo observed before he took a bite of his apple.

Breathing heavily, Roberto stepped back from the figure tied to the chair in front of him. "Yeah well, he fucking deserved it." Roberto staggered over to the table at the side of the room and grabbed a bottle of water, slugging at least half in one go. "Why the fuck can we not find anything on this fucking IEH? There's nothing, not a place of business, no name associated to it, nothing! They write their shit about me and post it on every goddamn social media platform in the city, and no one can trace it back to anyone!" He pointed at the bloodied corpse on the chair. "Not even the world's leading authority on cyber tracking can tell me who the fuck these bastards are!"

Vincenzo shrugged his shoulders. "Either the people on the streets don't know, or they are protecting IEH, which makes no fucking sense at all. We have made it very clear that what we are doing is in retaliation for those messages, but still no names."

Roberto picked up a towel and wiped the blood from his hands and removed the plastic apron he'd worn to protect his clothes. "Then concentrate on the redhead. IEH talks about stopping me at all costs, and she is out there doing everything she can. If anyone knows who they are, it will be her. And as for those fucking cats, I want them gone before Luciano arrives. He needs to see that I have full control of Chicago. We need to start rounding those fucking animals up and putting them out of my misery."

****

Mason lay still, watching his mate as she lay in his arms staring out at the rain falling steadily outside.

The lights from the city beyond her window reflecting in each drop as it slid down the panes of glass. By rights, she should be unconscious or at the very least asleep. He had lost count of the number of times he or Jacob had reached for her during the night. Violet had pleased both of them by doing her fair share of the reaching too.

They had even shifted for her to show her their leopards, and Mason had felt his animal's pride at being petted by their mate. The damn cat preened at all the attention and grumbled heartily when Mason forced him back and reclaimed his skin.

But now, when the dawn was about to break on a new day, their mate lay quietly between them, and he didn't need to be psychic to know she was thinking about her father. Hell, he had been all she'd thought about for the past twelve years as far as he could tell.

He caught Jacob's eye where he lay behind their mate, and could see the concern he felt mirrored in his brother's eyes. Violet was too quiet.

"You want to tell us what's going through that beautiful head of yours?" Mason decided to ask and just see how she reacted. The fact she didn't flinch or jump at his voice told him that she was more than aware of the fact that he and Jacob were awake, too.

"I was thinking about the moment my Poppa was killed," Violet said in a small quiet voice, and Mason desperately wanted to retract his question, but knew she probably needed to talk it through with them.

"How old were you when you lost him?" Jacob asked, and Violet tensed between them.

"I didn't lose him, he was taken from me," Violet's voice was flat and sounded devoid of emotion, which was a stark contrast to the tension in her body. "I was born Isabela Inez Santiago, but from the moment he saw me, my Poppa called me *Viola*. When Santiago learned I had a gift with computers, he brought in the best tutors to ensure I could write code that would be unbeatable, and from the age of ten that was what I did. I trained to fight, and I kept Santiago's wealth secure.

"When I was twelve, my father decided I needed to know what it was like to kill a man." Mason filled with horror and his leopard snarled and began to pace within him. "He told me that I needed to know what it was like to see someone die in front of me, and know what it is like to take a life." Violet took a deep shuddering breath before she continued. "But because my father is a sadistic son of a bitch, he wanted to make sure that I felt the loss as well."

"Fuck," Mason growled, his leopard very much in his voice. "Please tell me that fucker didn't make you kill your own grandfather!"

"He tried," Violet whispered. "He made me stand there with a gun in my hand, pointing it at the one man who had shown me nothing but kindness and love. Poppa had been trying to work out a way to get me away from my father, but Santiago had become too fucking rich and powerful. He had come to the house to try and reason with Santiago. Hell, he had even tried to appeal to my mother. But all he got for is trouble was a beat down from Santiago's right hand asshole, taken to a derelict house and then made to kneel with his hands tied behind his back facing his grandchild, who held a weapon on him."

"But you couldn't do it," Jacob said confidently.

Mason nodded. "You might have only been twelve, but there is no way in hell you would have pulled that trigger."

Violet relaxed a little between them. "Thanks for saying that, and you're right. I couldn't do it. And to punish me for my disobedience, Santiago had me beaten and—" Violet swallowed audibly, and a tendril of dread uncurled within him. "He had me raped in front of my Poppa." Twin growls filled the room, and Mason had to fight to keep his leopard from bursting free in need of vengeance. From the way Jacob's eyes were completely amber, Mason knew he, too, was fighting his animal for control.

"My Poppa fought hard to get to me, begging my father to stop it, and promising him anything and everything, but Santiago didn't care. Not about me, or my Poppa," Violet's voice shook, and Mason pressed harder against her. "While I lay there, trying desperately to distance myself from what was happening to me, I watched my Poppa. I kept my eyes on him. Even after Santiago put a bullet in his head, I never took my eyes from him."

Mason pressed soft kisses to her temple, moving gently to her cheek, gently sipping the tears that fell from her face. Jacob leaned down and placed gentle kisses on her bare shoulder. Mason's leopard pushed itself against him, trying to comfort their mate with touch.

"How did you get away?" Jacob asked quietly.

Violet took another shuddering breath and exhaled sharply. "When I was finally allowed to get up from the floor, the man who had raped me, my father, and the two guards who had stood by and let it happen, all stood around laughing at me. I was shaking, and as I struggled to pull the ripped shreds of my nightgown back together, my mind suddenly cleared. Their laughter flipped a switch within me, and I went from being a traumatized little girl, to a pissed off one in seconds. I dropped the nightgown, and grabbed the gun I had been given. I had a split second to choose who to shoot first, and what had just happened to me took precedence. Rather than put a bullet in Santiago, I shot the prick who had raped me. Then I turned, aimed, and fired at Santiago next, but there were no more bullets in the gun. Vincenzo's was fully loaded." Violet pressed her hand to her chest, right over the vicious scar they had discovered earlier. "They lit the house and left me in it to die, but I managed to get into the alley."

Mason's rage was a living, breathing thing within him. His leopard was roaring its rage, and he wanted to go out into the night and hunt every single one of those fuckers down. He would rip their hearts from their bodies, and his leopard would dine on them at the feet of their mate. Violet must have sensed his rage, one he knew that Jacob shared because she began to pet both of them, calming them with her touch as no other could.

"Violet." His voice trembled on her name.

"Shhh, I know," she whispered before leaning up and pressing a kiss to his lips, then turning to lie flat and press a kiss to Jacob's. Mason saw the tears on his brother's face, and in that moment became aware that he, too, was crying silently. "I survived, spent two years as a ward of the state while I siphoned cash from Santiago, using a few back doors in the systems I built for him, and I covered my tracks. Eventually I think he caught on that someone was doing it though, because he changed his entire financial system. I had enough to start though, and I used that and worked to get into a position where I could finally do what I couldn't do twelve years ago. I have the resources and I have the skill to take him down, and that is exactly what I am going to do."

"And you won't be doing it alone," Mason promised.

Violet looked up at him, and her gaze locked to his in the early morning light. "I'm not sure I know how to work as a team."

"Learn," Jacob said from behind her. "Santiago is

already dead. He just hasn't stopped breathing yet. When he does, we will be standing right beside you."

Violet's expression turned slightly wicked. "You know, he has a fear of shifters. Something happened when he was younger and he believes them to be possessed by demons."

Mason grinned. "Good to know! So we will be standing beside you in leopard form, with lions and tigers all positioned behind you. Fucker might think we are possessed by demons now, but by the time he takes his last breath, he'll think he's faced the devil himself."

Violet grinned obviously liking the sound of that. "Alpha kitty will love that, for sure. Now, enough of all this. I do not want my final memory of the first night we are together to be about my fucked up father." Violet launched herself up and over him, and Mason grinned as he gripped her hips and helped position her over his suddenly thick erection.

"What did you have in mind, little one?" Mason reached up and ran his hands over her breasts, squeezing and pulling her nipples, reveling in her mewl of pleasure and the way she wriggled her hips against him.

Violet's eyes darkened. "I want to fuck you." Mason was all aboard with that plan. "And I want to do that while I have Jacob in my mouth." From the way Jacob practically flew into a kneeling position beside them, Mason knew he was just as eager to put her plan into action as he was.

Mason lay back and let his mate have her way with him. There would be plenty of time to think about Santiago and make plans for his downfall later. Right now it was all about their mate, and giving her what she needed. His last thought before she took him into her body and he lost the ability to form coherent sentences, was that he hoped that he and Jacob could be what she needed for the rest of her life. Because she most definitely was for him.

Chapter Ten

"*Umph!* Fuck!"

Violet huffed a laugh as she wiped away the sweat from her forehead. "Awww, sorry, kitty cat, did that hurt? You are sounding a little frustrated."

Jacob flipped back up onto his feet. "Not at all, baby, just wanting to make sure you feel like you have a chance." He turned toward her and started side stepping, advancing and retreating in the methodical way a trained martial artist did.

Violet laughed out loud as she began matched every step with her own, the two of them circling each other around the padded gym mats in her dojo. "I do thank you for your consideration, and it might be more believable if I weren't beating your ass four falls to two. One more and you have to wash my back in the shower."

Jacob's grin was wicked. "You say that like it is a punishment. If anything it's an incentive just to throw the damn bout."

Violet grinned back, her eyes narrowing slyly. "True, but I reckon your competitive streak is too wide to simply roll over and play dead now, isn't it, kitty?"

Jacob winked at her, and then lunged forward so quickly it was instinct more than anything else that saved her, and had her leaping out of range in time. Violet couldn't remember having more fun working out. Mason and Jacob had both been keen to spend some time in her gym and dojo, and she had welcomed the opportunity to spar when Jacob offered.

Mason was out with Kieran, and the two of them would be back in a few hours. It was nice having one on one time with Jacob though. Her mind filled with some ideas of what they could be doing one on one and she decided it was time to end this and move on to more enjoyable endeavors.

She reached over her shoulder and grabbed a handful of the large t-shirt she wore, and tugged it over her head. "I'm getting a little warm."

Jacob's eyes dropped to her bra-clad breasts. "By all means, be comfortable."

With effort, Jacob lifted his gaze to meet hers, and she stepped forward, making sure to put a little more bounce in her step, and sure enough, Jacob's gaze dropped a second time. She stepped again, and Jacob's gaze stayed on her chest and she knew she had him.

Pushing up from the ground with both feet, she leaped at him, her right leg tucking into his stomach, her left into his back. With little more than a twist of her hips, and her momentum and she had him on the ground.

"Hi-yah!" She yelled her *kiai* as she lifted her right leg up and pretended to drop it on his sternum. She sat up, grinning at Jacob, who was looking up at her with a mock glare.

"I should call foul on that one, you know," Jacob complained as he rolled to the side and held out a hand to pull her to her feet.

"Any advantage necessary," Violet said with a grin, stepping into him and wrapping her arms around his waist. "I have a competitive streak a mile long as well, and I am not above using what the good Lord gave me in order to win."

Jacob smiled gently as he reached out and swept her hair from her face. "And I have to say he did a fan-fucking-tastic job in creating you, too, woman." His expression turned serious, and Violet had the very real feeling of drowning in his beautiful grey eyes. "Thank you for trusting us last night. Not just by giving yourself to us, but for telling us about your past. I know that wasn't easy for you, hell, it wasn't easy hearing it and not running out to cut the fucker then and there, fortified compound or not. But knowing that you have that much trust in us is humbling."

Violet felt herself blushed so pressed her face into his muscled chest. "As strange as it sounds, I do. Please don't hurt me." Those last four words were whispered, and she hadn't even realized she was going to say them, and she desperately wished she could take them back when she felt Jacob tense.

He gently gripped her shoulders and tugged her from his chest so he could look into her eyes. "Violet, there is no way Mason or I would or could ever hurt you. You are our *mate*. Ours to love, ours to cherish, and ours to protect from now until forever. I know you don't see that yet, but you will. Someday."

Violet didn't know what to say. She'd never had anyone tell her they would love, cherish, and protect her. Not even her Poppa. She had no words to tell him what he and Mason meant to her, so she pushed up onto her tiptoes reached up to wrap a hand around his neck, and tugged him down to meet her kiss.

She poured everything she could into that kiss. Her heart, her soul, every emotion she was feeling, she tried to convey through the passion she had for him. Jacob groaned into her mouth, wrapping his arms around her waist, and lifting her off the ground. Violet lifted her legs and wrapped them around his waist as he walked over to the door that led down to the apartment, never breaking the kiss.

When her need for air had her pulling back she was surprised to see that they were walking into her master bathroom. "I believe," Jacob's voice was deeper than usual, and she shivered at the timbre of his tone, "that I lost our little bet, and it's time I paid up."

Jacob walked to the shower, and turned it on

before setting her on her feet, and claiming her mouth with his own. He started out slow, taking his time until she felt completely taken over. Then as soon as she was completely compliant and under his spell, he changed the angle of the kiss and possessed her. All she could do was lean into him, hold on tight to his waist, and let him take her over. When Jacob pulled back she whimpered at the loss.

"Hop in, baby," Jacob said against her neck before he turned her to the shower and helped her in. She was shocked to discover that somehow he had managed to strip her bra, panties, and her yoga pants from her without her being aware.

She stepped under the stream of hot water and moaned at the spread of heat through her shoulders and back. When she turned, the sight of Jacob pulling off his shorts and walking toward her naked, erect, and the picture of hotness, heat spread through her entire body, pooling low in her abdomen.

When he stepped into the shower with her, she ran her hands down over his chest and abs, reveling in how the muscles beneath the skin jumped under her fingers. "I love how strong you and Mason are. You are both exquisite works of art, simply beautiful. If I could paint, I would want to paint the two of you, naked." She lifted her gaze from his chest to his face and saw a wash of color across his cheeks. "Are you blushing?"

"No," he was quick to deny, but his gaze flicked away and she grinned.

"You are. Is it because I find you beautiful?"

Jacob groaned at her teasing and leaned in to nip at her bottom lip, making her laugh.

"Would it make it better if I changed that to wanting to paint you both in chocolate body paint and lick it off?"

From the way amber filtered into Jacob's eyes and his erection bobbed between them, she knew he preferred that. Hell, she was pretty taken with that thought, too. She dropped to her knees before him. "But then again, who needs chocolate?"

She reached out and gripped his cock, loving the feel of the hard strength of it beneath the satin softness of his skin. She slid her hand up and down his shaft with the firm grip she knew her men preferred. With his body protecting her from the spray of the shower, she looked up to stare into his eyes. She leaned in, flicking her tongue over the slit at the head of his cock, delighting in his shiver and the way he bit his bottom lip.

Unable to hold back any longer, she leaned in and pulled him deep into her mouth, sucking hard and sliding the flat of her tongue along the sensitive underside.

"Goddamn it, Violet," Jacob groaned. "Fuck, that feels good."

She maintained a steady rhythm, using her mouth, her tongue and a decent amount of suction to drive him crazy. She wasn't able to take all of him into her mouth, so used her left hand on his shaft and her right hand cupped his balls and rolled them in her palm. Within minutes Jacob was growling constantly, a few colorful curses echoing around the shower walls, and she felt his hips starting to jerk forward as if unconsciously seeking the release she knew was building within him.

"Fuck, Violet," Jacob rasped reaching down to pull her up. "As amazing as it would be to come like that, I need to be inside you."

Violet was in complete agreement, and when Jacob lifted her, and pressed her back against the tiled wall of the shower, she wrapped her legs around his waist, reached down to align his cock with her pussy, and pulled him close. He slid to the hilt in one swift thrust, and both of them moaned at the feeling.

"So hot, so wet," Jacob murmured as he ran his hands down her arms to her hands, and lifted them above her head. "Hold on, baby, this is gonna go hard and fast." Then true to his word, Jacob started to move, pounding into her.

Pinned as she was to the wall, she was completely at his mercy. It was one of the hottest experiences of her life. To be fucked against the wall, staring into the eyes of the man pounding into your body, and knowing you could do nothing to prevent the orgasm racing toward you like a tsunami was heady stuff.

Violet inhaled sharply when her release suddenly slammed into her, and she screamed Jacob's name as her body shook and shuddered with pleasure. She managed to keep her eyes open, and witnessed the moment Jacob surrendered to his own release. His roar rang with hers filling the bathroom with the sounds of their joint passion. She flexed her hands in his, and as soon as he released her wrists, she reached her arms around him and gripped him tightly to her. The past forty-eight hours had been an emotional roller coaster, with her ripping her past open to Jacob and Mason, and for the first time in her life, she felt hopeful about her future.

Oh, she was still hell bent on the vengeance owed to her, but she was hopeful nonetheless.

Chapter Eleven

The scene unfolding on the screen before him was jumpy, but the quality was high and the image was clear. It showed two people standing in a darkened hallway talking quietly together. Although the video footage was high quality, the sound was poor. They couldn't hear what they were talking about, but their faces were clear despite the poor lighting.

And it was one face in particular that had Santiago's blood running cold, then burning hot with rage. "*Figlio di troia!*"

"Well, lookie who it is," Vincenzo said. "It appears the prodigal daughter didn't die in that damn fire like we thought, huh?"

Santiago roared, tempted to throw the tablet against the wall. "That fucking bitch is alive! Her hair is different, but no one could hide those eyes. It all makes fucking sense now. Who else has the skills to take every fucking software contract right out from under me? That fucking bitch owes me millions!"

Vincenzo nodded. "Yep, it would appear my shot wasn't as deadly as we thought. Surprising really. But you gotta admire her strength. You always thought that the person behind IEH and their single-minded focus to fuck you over had to be someone from your past, and someone who hated you. Well, you were right on both counts. There is no one in the world that has more right to hate you than that little girl, and I can't blame her."

Roberto spun on Vincenzo with a snarl. "I did nothing but teach that bitch that life was hard and she needed to fight. And how did she thank me? She has stolen from me. She fucking shot at me. At me! Her father!"

Vincenzo raised a brow at him. "There was no

bullet in the gun, to be fair. And you tried to get her to shoot her own grandfather. You had her beaten and raped in front of him, and then you shot him in the head while she watched. I really think—"

Boom!

Roberto waited for the rapport of the weapon he'd just fired to dissipate. Two more of his guards ran into the room, guns drawn, eyes casting about the room looking for the threat.

"Boss, you okay?"

Roberto nodded at the guard who asked the question and laid his gun back on the table. "I'm not sure if anyone else was getting sick of that bastard and his chatter, but I'd had enough of hearing what that fucker thought." He moved around Vincenzo, who had crumpled to the floor, blood oozing onto the concrete floor from the whole where his face used to be. "Take care of that mess and then head out into the city. I need you to pick something up for me."

The older of the guards looked up, his face unchanged by the gore and horror that lay at his feet. "What might that be, boss?"

Roberto handed him the tablet and pointed to the screen. "Her."

****

"How's the miracle cure working out for Alpha Kitty?" Violet said into the phone, grinning when Mason chuckled.

"Why do you assume it was Kieran that tried it out and not one of us?" Mason asked, humor clear in his tone.

"Puh-lease. That man would never allow one of his pride to take a chemical cocktail and then take a bullet to see if it worked. Was it you that got to shoot him? You do realize that it should have been me. I was the one that broke down the compounds on Santiago's bullets and it was me that worked out the correct steroid and desmopressin levels to get your blood clotting in order to counteract his shitty bullets. I should have been the one to shoot him."

Violet heard a male voice in the background, but couldn't make out what they said. Mason laughed again down the phone. "Kieran is close enough to have heard what you said and he's afraid where you might have actually placed that bullet."

"In his ass of course," Violet sing-songed back.

This time there was a distinct feline growl in the background and that she heard perfectly. "Before you get yourself into even more trouble with my Alpha, my love, I will tell you that your little chemical cocktail worked perfectly. He bled a little more than we normally would have, but he is healing as we speak. Jacob is distributing the rest of the stuff you gave us to the other pride members who came out to watch."

Violet grinned. "Wait, you all went out into the woods to watch a lion get shot? What is it a slow day in the pride house today or what?"

"Probably had more to do with the money we all had on whether Kieran could control his animal enough not to strike back at the lucky bastard who did get to shoot him."

"And? Don't stop there. The anticipation is killing me."

"Well, I'm still alive and talking to you on the phone, so it worked out."

Violet giggled, a sound she had never heard from herself a week ago, before she'd met her two leopards that now meant more to her than she ever thought anyone would. "Although I'm glad you're okay, kitty cat, I do have to protest the fact that you got to shoot Alpha Kitty and I didn't."

The vibration at her wrist signaled she had a message, and she frowned when she read the origin. Josie Cadman was messaging her again, and that could mean more of Santiago's men or Diablo's gang were heading back into her neighborhood. Violet stood up from her couch and headed for her study.

"How far away are you?"

"About an hour from you," Mason answered immediately, no thread of the humor from moments before in his tone. "We're not far from the pride house. Why, what's going on?"

Violet sat at her desk and fired up her computer. "It could be nothing, but Josie is reaching out again." She clicked on the message icon that flashed in the corner of her screen.

"Isabella," Violet gasped at the sound of her father calling her name. "I know it's you." Her entire body turned cold, her heart pounded within her chest and she started to shake uncontrollably. "There is no deeper betrayal than that of a daughter who turns on her own father. The thought that it is you behind this IEH simply turns my stomach. Everything you are, everything you have become is because of me. I helped bring you into this world, and by God, I am going to be the hand of vengeance that takes you out of it!

"I want what's owed me. You have stolen millions from me over the years, and I know you've made even more with what you stole. You will come to me, and you will transfer everything you have back to me. With interest. I have the woman you were expecting to hear from. We are in the warehouse built over the house I thought we'd killed you in. You have forty-five minutes from the time I send this message to get here otherwise I will turn her over to my men and let them do with her what they will. Then, once she is all healed up again, I am sure I will find a willing buyer for her. She's young and spirited. I bet she'll like it." Violet heard Josie cry out in pain in the background. "You know exactly how that feels now don't you, *figlia?* If you do not come, no matter, it is only matter of time until I find you. I know that you have been working with that fucking abomination and his *pride.*" Santiago practically spat that word, his distaste and hatred obvious in his tone. "I am looking forward to ending those demons in a very bloody way soon. And of course I am anxious for *our* reunion. I know it was you that has killed many of my men, and I must say that perhaps I misjudged you. Perhaps you are more like your father than I thought. Now, come to me, you little bitch."

The message ended, and Violet checked the date code on the message. Seven-sixteen PM. A quick look at the clock in the corner told her she only had forty minutes left.

"Violet!" She jolted at the sound of Mason's voice coming from the forgotten phone still clutched in her hand. "We're already on our way, love. Wait for us. We'll go together."

Violet heard the noise in the background and knew Mason was running through the forest. He was an hour away. If they broke every speed limit between her and the pride house then they *might* make it in time, but there were no guarantees. She stood up, embracing the ice that still flowed through her, and walked toward her elevator.

"Mason, you know I have to go." She pressed the button on the lift doors. "It's what us good Samaritans do."

"Fuck, Violet, please just wait!" Mason was yelling and running at the same time. Violet could hear the growls and roars of his pride that obviously ran with him.

"I can't wait. Don't come here when you get into the city. Find me in the warehouse district, on Lake Street," Violet took a deep breath. "I love you, Mason, you and Jacob. No matter what, I need you to know that." Her voice broke on her last word.

"Goddamn it, Violet, I love you, too." Violet heard the desperation in his tone, and knew the growl of pain that sounded somewhere near him had to be Jacob. She hoped he'd heard her.

"I would have loved being your mate in truth," she whispered then disconnected the phone, turning it off immediately. She stepped into the lift and pressed her hand against the wall. By the time the doors opened into her lab, she was completely under control. Well, if she ignored the single tear that fell unchecked down her cheek. And she was determined to do just that.

****

"I would have loved being your mate in truth."

Jacob felt like he was being shredded from the inside out as his mind replayed those words over and over. She was everything he had ever hoped for in the woman the Fates had deemed them worthy of. To hear the sadness in her tone, and the goddamn fear he knew she would be horrified to know he'd caught to, slew him. He pushed his leopard even faster through the forest, the trees blurring as he ran past them. Mason ran beside him having shifted as soon as the phone call had ended.

He slid to a halt when they reached the jeeps, and he shifted, the change painful as his leopard fought it for the first time. Both animal and man wanted to be there for their mate. Jacob reached for the driver's side door handle of the closest jeep, but when he opened the door, Kieran climbed into the seat.

"Oh hell, no," Jacob snarled, reaching a hand out with the intention of ripping his Alpha from the seat, but was stopped by a quick sharp jab to the nose. "What the fuck, Kieran! My mate is heading into danger, and you drive like you're driving Miss Daisy. Get the fuck out of the seat."

Kieran's growl was filled with dominance, but in his panic and fear for his mate, Jacob withstood dropping to his knee, but he did tilt his head in submission. "We need to get there in once fucking piece, Jacob. Now, get your ass in the car, put the fucking shorts on that are back there, and then hold the hell on."

"Damn it all to hell," Mason growled as he clambered into front passenger seat of the jeep, and Jacob flung himself into the back seat. "You think she'll go or will she do the smart thing and keep her ass safe until we can reach her?"

True to his word, Kieran slammed the jeep into gear, and left the parking lot in a hail of gravel and dust. "I don't know her as well as the two of you, but I am going to choose option number one. Your mate feels guilty for what her father has done in the past few years. If there is a chance, no matter how slight, that she might be able to save one person from him, then yeah, my guess she is heading in his direction as we speak."

Jacob was so damn anxious to get there it felt like a thousand tiny explosions were going off under his skin. "He only gave her forty-five minutes. We have less than thirty minutes to get to Lake Street. Can we make it?"

The jeep took a corner on what felt like two wheels and Kieran accelerated out of the corner like he was driving Formula One. The other two jeeps filled with feline shifters fell a little behind. "We'll be cutting it close."

Mason cursed. "We are at least forty minutes out,

Alpha."

"Bullshit," Kieran snapped, pulling as much speed from the jeep. "I have never let one of my pride down, and I sure as fuck do not mean to start today. I'll have us there in thirty."

Jacob hung on as tight as he could to the "oh shit" bar above his head, and prayed as hard as he could.

Chapter Twelve

Violet's stomach turned at the sound of flesh meeting flesh followed by Josie's whimpering sobs. All of it was coming from somewhere inside one of the sectioned off areas of the warehouse. The facility was large, and the ground floor had been partitioned to enable multiple uses of the space with walls and large double door openings, but no ceilings over the area. A series of catwalks bisected the building from one end to the other.

She had entered through one of the windows on the second floor, guessing that Santiago would have all the ground floor entrances covered. She crept along a catwalk near the roof of the warehouse, trying as desperately as possible to stick to the shadows.

She came to the part of the catwalk that looked down over the area her father stood, watching as one of his men slapped the young woman around. Josie was tied to a chair and had no hope of blocking or hiding from the punishing slaps, and from how swollen and bloody her face was, they had been doing it for a while. A quick glance around the area told her there were four of her father's guards in the room with her father, and two standing on the other side of the entry.

"How does it feel to know that you are about to die?" Her father's voice came from below her, and it was filled with a smug satisfaction. "Many people often wonder what it will feel like to die, when will the reaper come for them and where in their life will they be. Now, you have the answer to all but one of those questions."

"But I don't want to know the answer to any of those questions!" Josie cried out, her voice trembling.

Santiago made a scoffing noise. "Bullshit! Everybody wants to know the answer to that question. It is the very unknown that is faced by all species. When will I die?"

"Hopefully today, you narcissistic motherfucking son of a bitch!" Josie screamed back, and even from where Violet stood at least twenty feet away from her, she could see the hate burning bright in the young woman's eyes. "You and your filth disgust me. You think just because you have money and power that you can buy yourselves respect and honor. Well, wise up and smell the fucking coffee, you dumbass. Fear is not respect. Power is not honor. And I may not live to see the day when some lucky bastard ends your pitiful life, but I can assure you that I will be cheering that person on all the way from heaven. I'll be popping popcorn and waiting as you descend to the depths of hell to be ass-fucked by the devil himself!"

Violet blinked and a slow smile formed. She had only known Josie a short time, and in those months, if anyone had asked Violet to give them a word that described her, she would have had to say timid. Where this eyes blazing, mouth like a sailor on shore leave, spitfire came from, Violet couldn't tell, but she liked it!

When Santiago backhanded Josie this time, the whimper she gave was more a growl of hatred, and she spat blood in his direction.

Good girl!

Santiago cursed and reached for a handkerchief. "Spit at me all you want, bitch. My clients prefer a little fire with their purchase. They will soon break you of that and we may start early with that if my disloyal daughter is not here in the next three minutes."

Violet closed her eyes for a moment, knowing that as soon as she slid down the ladder beside her, and entered into the pit of snakes below, she would be forfeiting her life. And up until meeting Jacob and Mason that might not have been as horrific a thought as it was now. She let memories of their brief time together filter through her mind, remembering what it was to be held by them, to laugh with them, and to be loved by them.

She loved them with everything in her, and she knew they loved her right back. All three of them had spoken the words, and Violet knew that it didn't matter that they weren't mates in the true sense of the word. The connection between them was such that if the situations were reversed and they were facing their own end, she would likely follow them into the next life, unprepared to brave the future of this one without them. Oh, she would hang on a little longer and wait until she have wrought justice on anyone who dared to take her mates from her, but she would follow them eventually.

They were her mates.

Violet felt a sudden sharp pain in her chest, a burning sensation that seemed to escalate in intensity until her eyes watered and she had to take shallow breaths to keep from crying out. Then just as quickly as it came, it disappeared, and she knew it had happened. The mating bond between her and her leopards had snapped into place. Just as they had explained, in the moment when she accepted what they were to her, and she to them, the connection between them would be forged.

She panted for breath for a moment longer, her palm pressed to where the ache in her chest had been. She could feel the connection taking hold within her. She sensed Jacob and Mason's joy that the bond had snapped into place, but she also felt their fear for her, their determination to get to her in time, and their trepidation that they might be too late. Although the feelings that came to her were most definitely shared by both men, she sensed Mason's ice cold determination, and Jacob's heated rage, and she knew she would always feel their emotions separately along the bond. Violet tried to send them her love as well as her plea that they forgive her for making this decision. She could only hope that somehow they understood that she was doing what she had to, and there was no other choice. Not for her.

They would find each other in the next life, and every one after it. Of that she had no doubt. Feeling the sands of time slipping way too damn fast, Violet opened her eyes, turned and grabbed the handles of the ladder that ran from the catwalk to the floor below. The bottom of the ladder would put her only fifteen feet from where Santiago stood over Josie. She placed her feet on either side and slid down the rails of the ladder to the floor.

"Well now, it looks like you started the party without me." She spoke as she turned to face the man who had sired her, and leaned back against the ladder. She kept her eyes on Santiago and ignored the other men in the room who all raised semi-automatic weapons in her direction.

Santiago grinned as folded his arms across his chest and stared at her. "I never said she'd be unharmed when you got here, just that she would be alive. For now at least."

Violet stared at the man who had been responsible for every fucked up nightmare and fear she had. The irony was she felt no real emotion looking at the man now. Sure he looked the same, just slightly rounder and greyer, but the hard, evil stare was still there, as was the disapproving scowl when he looked at her. But something had changed in the twelve years since she'd stood before the man, and it was obvious to her what it was. She was no longer that scared little girl anymore.

Violet grinned as she pushed to stand upright and moved away from the ladder. "That's true, you didn't, and even if you had promised, I wouldn't have believed you. I reckon it would be too hard for a lying sack of shit like yourself to actually keep your word. Hell, the ground might even open up and swallow you whole. No doubt the hordes in hell would welcome the return of their brother from another mother." She shot a quick glance at Josie. "The ass-fucking would no doubt start soon after."

Josie huffed a tired laugh. "Then hell, you had better get me out of this chair so I can get to popping us that popcorn."

Totally ignoring Josie, Santiago's eyes narrowed on Violet, and she smiled sweetly, reveling in the flush of anger that rose in his face. "It would appear my sniveling little bitch has found a backbone. When you were a child, you never would have said such things to your father. You would have been more likely to stand in the corner and cry. But look at you now. I know that you've killed, and you've fought to fuck up my business dealings all around the world, and for the first time in my life I have never been prouder of you, Isabella."

"Aw, isn't that sweet." Violet folded her arms, slipping two of her shock buttons from the specially designed compartment in the arms of her fight suit and palming them. "The irony is, if I had known my successful attempts to take business from you and make you look like a horse's ass to the international business community would actually make you proud of me, I might have actually thought twice about it!"

"Shut your mouth, whore!" One of her father's guards jumped to his defense and stepped forward, his hand moving up with the intent of back handing her across the face. Violet waited until his arm was swinging toward her before she spun into him, putting her back to his chest, and slapping both of her shock buttons on his thighs. She felt him jolt behind her before she turned quickly to drive the elbow of her right arm into his temple.

Without so much as a groan, the man slid to the floor, and Violet spun low, on the balls of her feet, waiting to see if any of the others came at her.

Santiago's smile broadened. "Look at that. You moved without telegraphing your intention. You have learned a lot in the last twelve years."

Violet shrugged and straightened, moving back slightly to give herself some room. "So, you wanted me here, and I came. Are you going to let Josie go? I'm pretty sure the answer is no." Violet winced at being so blunt. "Yeah, sorry, Josie, but Santiago never had any intention of letting you go. You were just the bait to get me here."

Josie nodded, her face filled with resignation. "I reckon I've been living on borrowed time for a while now, so all good."

Santiago nodded, his expression turning smug. "You're right. No intention whatsoever to let the bitch walk out of here alive, but I do have to ask you, Isabella, knowing that by coming here you were simply rushing the inevitable and dying at my hand, why the hell did you come?"

Violet grinned, reveling in Santiago's expression morphing to one of confusion. "Because you stupid son of a bitch, you live in a fortified fortress, and on those rare occasions you left, you would travel with so many guards it's impossible to get near you. This way, here you stand, with only three men standing between me and you, and because you are an arrogant prick who thinks he can counter anything, you believe yourself infallible. I came because I made a promise to myself twelve years ago that I would end you by any means and at any cost. Today I make good on that oath." A wave of bloodlust and relief flooded the mating bond. Her mates were close

Santiago's face filled with thunder. "You think a

pathetic little whore like you can stop me? I am Roberto Santiago!"

"And you killed my Poppa. Prepare to die," Violet paused for a moment. "What, no one gets that reference? *Princess Bride,* people! Jesus, Santiago, what kind of idiots have you hired?" The three guards in the room shuffled forward, no doubt taking offense at her calling them idiots, but hey, she called a spade a spade.

"Maybe you are less like me than I thought," Santiago snarled. "That incessant and irrelevant babbling is more like your fucking mother than me."

Violet grinned. "It's not incessant babbling when I'm stalling for time, you douchebag." Kieran's loud and if she was not mistaken, extremely pissed off roar filled the air from just beyond the walls of the warehouse, followed by semi-automatic fire and the terrified screams of Santiago's men. "It would appear that the Black Ridge pride has come out to play, *Daddy dearest.*" Violet let her contempt for the man resonate in her tone.

Santiago made a hand signal, and the three men lifted their weapons and trained them on her. "That plays into my hand perfectly. Let them come and face my men. I look forward to watching them all bleed out."

"You are of course assuming that they are still susceptible to that chemical cocktail you had made. Time will tell I suppose." Violet let her gaze drift to the three men. "But, more importantly, how to fill in the time before the inevitable showdown, hmm?" Violet dropped down into a fighting stance, both hands going to the hand grips of her fighting batons behind her. "How about we have a little three on one action? What do you say, Santiago? You want to see just how much I've learned in the past twelve years?"

She watched as Santiago's eyes narrowed, and she could almost taste his arrogance. He no doubt believed the pride was being slaughtered beyond these walls, and he would get to watch his daughter being beaten on. "Three hundred thousand to each man if the bitch is taken alive. I want the money she owes me. If you have to kill her, do so, but you won't get a dime." All three of the guards grinned.

Santiago walked over to the entrance and spoke to the two guards standing there. "There's the same for you if you can keep all of those abominations out of this room until this is done."

Both guards nodded and lifted their weapons, completely focused on the halls that led to the area.

The three guards placed their weapons on the ground behind them, and moved forward, all three of them had smug looks on their faces, no doubt confident that three of them against one of her were even odds.

Violet kept her expression blank as the three came closer, calculating her next moves. The one the left was the strong looking of the three, but the guard on the right had a collection of tattoos across his throat and over his hands that screamed street gang. That meant street smarts. This one would fight hard and dirty to win. He was the first one she had to incapacitate. She knew that they would want to flank her and gain a tactical advantage that she couldn't allow them to gain.

Stepping forward, she drew out her batons, faked moving left then spun right, coming hard at the tattooed guard. She struck with calculated moves, driving the baton in her left hand into his upper arm. Then when he reached out with his left hand to reach for her, she brought her other baton down hard on his wrist she heard a satisfying crunch when it hit. She then slammed the baton in her left hand as hard as she could into his groin. The guy hunched over and dropped to the ground.

She groaned and leaned in against the body shot

the large fucker landed on her right side. She jumped back when he went to follow up with a second one, and ignoring the fire that was spreading up her side, spun her hand back to strike him in the jaw. Wanting to share the pain, she slammed her other hand out to catch the one in the middle square in the nose. She let loose with a flurry of baton strikes to both men countering and striking anywhere she could land a hit.

She had caught a couple of hard punches herself, and knew there was blood dripping down her chin from a lucky hit the guy in the middle managed to connect with during his random arm flailing, but nothing that was slowing her down too much. She landed a strike with the hilt of her baton to the temple of the largest bastard, and wanted to cheer when the guy dropped to the floor.

"Timber!" she called out as she turned to her last opponent. "That was totally appropriate right?" she asked the last guard left. "I mean that fucker was *big.* I mean like tree big. I don't know about you, but I felt the damn room shake when he hit the floor. Now, it's just you and me. One on one. *Mano a mano.* Just as the good Lord planned it." She spun her batons in her hands with the knowledge she was intimidating the hell out of the guy. "Let's end this so I can get some quality time with my dad."

Violet turned her head to look over at Santiago, and the smile that she'd worn slipped as she looked right down the barrel of the gun he was pointing in her direction. Violet had read once that no one actually sees the bullet that hits them, and she could honestly say that was true. She saw the moment the weapon was fired, but missed the bullet itself, but she sure as fuck felt it when it struck her in the side. Whether by accident or intent, the bastard had managed to hit one of the few areas of the suit that had no Kevlar.

As she spun with the momentum of the bullet and stumbled backward she kept her feet beneath her by sheer will alone. She refused to fall, knowing that if she did it would all be over. She felt the mating bond throb with equal parts concern for her, and rage at Santiago. She breathed deep as she fought the wave of nausea the came with the white-hot pain in her side, and from the wet feel of warmth sliding down over her hip and thigh, she knew she was bleeding heavily. That didn't bode well, really.

"Enough!" Santiago roared. "If you want something done right, then do it yourself." He lifted the weapon again, just as a cacophony of noise broke out just beyond the entrance to the room.

Amid the growls and roars of large cats, came the screams of men for a few brief moments, before they ended on strangled cries. A leopard walked into the room, and she knew from seeing him fight in that form that it was Jacob who stalked into the room in his leopard form, the spotted fur crimson around his jaw and front paws. Jacob had a bullet wound to his flank, but the bleeding had already stopped. She saw Santiago stare at the wound in confusion, then looked down at the gun he carried.

There was a blur at the door, and then the third and final guard that had been staring at Jacob in horror screamed in pain and terror as Mason took him down. Her leopard dispatched the man quickly, and then his huge head spun in Santiago's direction, hatred blazing in his eyes as the blood from his latest kill still dripped from his jaws.

Violet huffed out a pained laugh. "Perhaps your earlier assumption regarding your impending victory was a little premature." The growls rumbled continuously and filled the room as Jacob and Mason stalked towards her, their eyes never leaving Santiago.

Violet looked over at the man and saw fear shining in his eyes, the weapon now alternating between Jacob and Mason, but the hand that held it shook. "Santiago, I would like to introduce you to my mates." Jacob and Mason moved to stand beside her. Perhaps they sensed her growing weakness or they simply needed to feel her close. Either way they pressed against her legs and she dropped her hands to their backs. They had to be at least a meter tall at their shoulders, and their presence lent her courage and strength.

Santiago scowled. "What does that mean? You've given yourself to these abominations? Are you their bitch?"

Violet smiled, knowing it would enrage him further. "Aww, now see I thought you were brighter than that. Bitches are more of a dog thing than a cat thing."

"Still means you're sleeping with a fucking animal."

Violet nodded. "Not only that, I am fated to them both. They are both my mates, and I love them more than anything in the world."

"Love?" Santiago scoffed. "A frivolous emotion that means nothing! Power and money are the only currencies in this world that will get you anything or anywhere."

"That's where you are wrong." Violet turned as a shadow neared the door. "Dominance gets you pretty damn far in life, too. I have one more person to introduce you to. Santiago, this is Kieran."

A giant white lion stepped into the room. Like her mates, he sported blood around his jaw, his huge paws and there was more than one bullet wound on the animal. The lion was larger than any lion she had seen in the zoo or on the Discovery Channel. He epitomized strength and power, and his gaze was locked on Santiago.

"Kieran Murphy, Alpha of the Black Ridge pride," Violet continued, "this is Roberto Santiago."

Violet heard a whimper of sound from Santiago, and it held a thread of emotion she had never heard from her father. Fear. Kieran threw back his huge head and roared his challenge to the world. The sound was so loud, Violet lifted her hands to her ears. Then he leaped toward Santiago just as her father lifted his weapon, but Kieran was so fast, he was only able to get a single round off. What followed was as disturbing as it was justified, and Violet stood tall and watched as the Black Ridge Alpha took the man responsible for a lot of horror in her life, out of the world.

When Santiago was dead, Kieran stood over him, blood dripping from his massive jaws and once again, threw his head back and roared. To Violet it was very clear that the emotion in this one was more triumphant and less challenging than the first. She wanted to point out to her mates that perhaps she was starting to learn to speak lion, but never got to tell them. The darkness that had been leeching into the sides of her vision suddenly closed in, and she was unconscious before she even knew she was going to pass out.

Chapter Thirteen

"So how are you really feeling, V?"

Violet grinned at the concerned look on Dot's face on the computer monitor. "Better than I ever have in some ways. Not having Santiago to piss off anymore is almost sad, but I am by no means saying I want the fucker back. I'm sure he's roasting in hell, and that is exactly where he should be."

Dot nodded and leaned back in her chair. "Truer words have never been spoken, and I look forward to seeing what you can do with IEH now that you are no longer just playing with Santiago, but there is something else going on here. You and I have talked every day in the last three weeks since you were released from the hospital, and this is the first day you seem more like your old self. What's happened?"

Violet felt heat sweep into her face. She had the go-ahead from her doctor this morning to resume all physical activity, and that meant she no longer just had to sit and take what her mates gave her, and she was determined to give as good as she got tonight. She just wasn't sure how to tell the woman she considered to be more her mother than the woman who had given birth to her, that she was happy and excited to be given the green light to take her mates the way she had been dreaming about.

"Ooo, now that is an interesting shade of red there, V," Dot teased, leaning closer to her monitor. "I am guessing from the heat in those cheeks, the doctor has given you some good news and you are about to jump Jacob and Mason's bones but good!"

Violet's jaw dropped. "Dot! What in the hell? The eighties called and they want their expression back."

Dot winked. "The expression might be dated, but

the meaning is still what it has always been. You've been given the go ahead to bump pelvises with those delicious mates of yours."

"Oh my God, woman, would you stop!"

"What? Bump pelvises? You don't like that one either? How about 'play a round of hide the hooded salami'?" Dot was grinning like a mad woman now, obviously extremely pleased with herself.

"Dot!" Violet warned, but she could hear the laughter in her voice.

"Swap bodily fluids? Bone? That one's still relevant right?"

"I'm signing off now, crazy woman."

"Give each other a little pickle tickle? Slam a home run?"

"Bye, Dot!" She reached for the key that would disconnect the call

"Or just a good old fashioned hard f—"

The screen went black, and Violet fell forward giggling. She was lucky to have such good friends, and Dot was definitely one of the best. She was also extremely fortunate to have the pride as family, and she had loved the conversations and verbal sparring she and Kieran had engaged in over the past weeks. Then there were Jacob and Mason, who were now living in her apartment with her, and she thanked God and every deity she knew for them every single day of her life.

Josie had spent some time in the hospital at the beginning of her stay, and Kieran had somehow wrangled it so that she and Violet shared a hospital room. Violet had enjoyed getting to know Josie, and they spoke every day now. She'd never had a BFF before. She was also enjoying how tongue-tied Joise got around a certain white lion Alpha Kitty, and if Violet wasn't wrong Kieran reacted just as much to Josie as she did him.

Her mating bond flooded with love, and need pulling her from her musings. Violet sat up as heat pooled within her in reaction. She quickly scanned the alarms and sensors around the apartment to ensure everything was safe, a habit she wasn't sure she would ever get over. They had removed the threat of Santiago, but Kieran was adamant there were others that would come to take his place.

She stood up from the desk and practically skipped out of the office, heading out to find her mates. She glanced out the window and sighed at the lights of Chicago flickering against the night sky then turned to see that all the lights in the living area had been turned off. Apparently they were all heading to bed early, and she was totally on board with that plan. Turning toward the door that led to the master suite she saw a sliver of warm light where the door had been left ajar.

Her heart rate increased as she walked quickly to the door. Inhaling, she caught the scent of lavender in the air, and knew her mates had lit the candles she had scattered around the room. Biting her lip as anticipation filled her she quietly opened the door and had to bite back a moan at the sight that greeted her.

Jacob stood leaning against the back wall, and Mason sat on the bed, his elbows resting on his knees. They were both barefoot and wearing nothing but a pair of low hung jeans, and both had their gazes locked to her. Never before had she understood the saying like a deer caught in headlights, but the hunger she read in their eyes and the heat that poured down their mating bond had her understanding it completely.

Her mouth dried up as she closed the door and leaned against it.

"Come here, little one." Holy hell, Mason's voice was at least an octave lower and completely off the panty-melting scale.

Attempting to channel one of those fluid dancers she'd seen on YouTube, she walked slowly in his direction, carefully placing one foot in front of the other and adding more than just a touch of hip to each step. When Mason's grin turned appreciative and she heard a growl of appreciation from Jacob she knew she'd pulled it off. This was good because she feared she might look less like a fluid dancer and more like a baby giraffe just finding its feet. Jacob moved from the wall, to step up behind her as she stopped just in front of Mason.

"I love these yoga pants and loose tops you wear," Mason said quietly as he reached out to wrap a hand around each of her thighs and tugged her to stand between his legs. "I know they must be comfortable for you, but they hug every delicious curve in the most delightful way."

Violet trembled when she felt Jacob move closer, and press up against her. "But when you are wearing nothing at all?" He tugged her loose shirt over her head, and both men moaned at the sight of her bare breasts below the shirt. "You are fucking phenomenal."

Jacob wrapped both his arms around her waist under her arms and reached up to cup her breasts. She moaned when he used the thumbs and forefingers of both hands to roll both her nipples between them.

She looked down when she noticed Mason had tensed, and saw his gaze locked to the sight of the bullet wound on her side. The bullet hadn't struck her anywhere life threatening, but because Santiago had coated it with that damn anticoagulant, she had bled a lot more than she had anticipated. When she had passed out in that warehouse, Jacob and Mason had been distraught and according to Kieran, hadn't calmed down until she'd opened her eyes again. And that wasn't until after surgery to remove the bullet and quite a few pints of blood to replace what she had lost.

"What's up, pussy cat?" she whispered and grinned when Mason scowled at her. "Oh, come on, I'm too damn cute to scowl at."

"Be that as it may, little one," Mason said as his gaze dropped to the wound and his hand reached out to touch it. "There is no laughing matter in this. You were shot. You bled in our arms, and that scar is an obscene reminder of that. It will take me a while to get used to seeing it marring your beautiful skin."

Violet rolled her eyes at him and put her hands on her hips. The move must have looked pretty funny because Jacob hadn't let go of her breasts. "Look, we need to get the hell over that and move on. Santiago shot me, he shot Jacob, his men shot the shit out of all of the Black Ridge Pride, and especially poor old Alpha Kitty, but we all lived to love another day. This day in particular. Now, I got the go-head from the doctor, and I want to make love. Are you feeling up to it, Mason, or is this going to be a one on one deal? Because as much as I love my one on one time with you both, I was really hoping for some double loving tonight."

Mason's expression turned wicked as he ran his hands to the waistband of her yoga pants, and tugged them down, dragging her panties with them. "Oh, little one, I think you'll find out very shortly that I am more than up for some double loving."

"Me too," Jacob rasped in her ear. "More than up to having you jump my bones."

Violet froze.

"Yep," Mason added as he leaned in and pressed a kiss to her tummy. "Let's bump pelvises."

"And play a round of hide the hooded salami," Jacob whispered, amusement in his tone.

"You eavesdropping little eavesdroppers," Violet said with a pout. "Man, I am going to have to lock my office door and install soundproof insulation from now on. Your shifter hearing is just too damn good!"

Jacob laughed as he swung her around to face him, and lifted her so that they were eye level. "Yeah, but where would the fun be in that? Mason and I were planning on running you a relaxing bath and maybe giving you a gentle massage until we found out you had the all clear from the doctor. Now? Well, let's just say that our plans have changed."

Violet leaned in and sucked his bottom lip into her mouth, making him moan before she released it with a pop. "Oh yeah? What's the plan now?"

Jacob slammed his mouth to hers, thrusting his tongue into her mouth and devouring her whimper of desire. He stoked the arousal spiraling within her in moments then pulled back to look at her, leaving both of them breathing slightly heavier. "Now, we are going to take you together, just like I know you've wanted for a long time."

Violet felt heat flood through her and pool between her thighs. "How would you know that?"

Jacob's eyes became hooded and he inhaled deeply. "Because your beautiful body tells us everything we need to know about what it is that you are wanting and how you want it. We've talked about it, and every time we do, your sweet, sweet body tells us that you want it."

Jacob placed her gently on the ground and turned her to face the bed. Mason was sitting back on the bed in all his naked glory, and his impressive erection stood up to attention against his muscular torso.

Violet giggled, and Mason's gaze narrowed on her. "You know little one, when a dominant male is lying naked in front of you, giggling is most definitely not the reaction he is expecting."

"I know, I know, but when I see you sitting there all naked and yummy I realize how ridiculous it is for me to call you kitty cat." Violet grinned as she stepped closer and moved to sit down on Mason's legs.

Mason widened his legs so that she had to shimmy forward. "So, does that mean you'll lose that ridiculous nickname?"

"Hell, no," Violet said with a laugh. "Why would I do that when I know it riles you up so pretty?"

Mason growled low in his chest, his eyes flickered amber but there was amusement and love radiating there. She reached out and took his cock in her hand, stroking him from root to tip with a strong hand, adding a twist at the top the way she knew he liked, and from the purr and growl that came from the big man, she knew he appreciated it.

"Don't tease me, love," Mason groaned. "All this talk of slamming in a home run with a little pickle tickle has me on the edge."

All three of them laughed, and Violet pushed up onto her knees, shuffling forward and let out a moan when Mason pulled her nipple into his mouth, drawing strongly on her. Reaching down she positioned the blunt head of his cock where she needed it most and slowly slid down his length, not stopping until she was settled completely on his lap, and she had every delectable inch of him.

"Well," she said in a sultry tone she never knew she had until she'd found her mates, "I don't want to keep you hovering on the edge for too long, not when I'm feeling all not and needy, too." Violet began to move on him, loving how his fingers convulsed on her hips when she took all of him.

"So fucking hot," Mason moaned. "So fucking wet."

Violet felt the tendril of her orgasm start to tighten with her, and she started to move a little faster. Jacob leaned over her shoulder, halting her upward movement. "Ah ah ah, not without me, my love," Jacob bit down on her shoulder, and she emitted a little whimper.

Mason groaned as he lay back, the muscles in his abs and torso standing out in stark relief at his move. "Jacob, you had better get her ready, I'm not sure how long I can last here."

Jacob pressed on Violet's back, and she leaned forward, not stopping until her arms were on the bed beside Mason's shoulders.

"Hey, beautiful girl," Mason whispered as he stared up at her, and she could not think of a time she'd felt more beautiful. She held herself still and groaned as Mason thrust up into her in a slow rhythm that created a steady burn within her.

"A little cold, baby," Jacob warned and then she felt him rubbing his fingers around her back entrance, easing lubrication around the tight ring of muscle and then pushing in. "That's it, baby. Damn, you look so fucking beautiful like this." She felt him scissoring his fingers within her, stretching her body to accommodate him, and she writhed at how good it felt. Oh, there was a burn to it, but it was one she knew she would quickly become addicted to.

"Yeah, you like that don't you, little one?" Mason whispered from beneath her. "I can feel your arousal building down the mating bond, but even if I couldn't you just covered my cock with your desire. Fuck, you are perfect for us. Just perfect."

Jacob's hand slipped away, and Violet felt the loss

for a moment, before he stepped back, this time much closer. "Here we go, baby, push out against me." His whisper sounded from behind her, and she felt the head of his cock press against her back entrance. Doing what he told her to do, she pushed out as he pushed in, forcing herself to relax and submit to him. "That's it," Jacob said in a strained voice. "You are doing so fucking well, so beautiful, there you got me, baby, you got all of me."

Violet let out the breath she hadn't realized she had been holding and focused on the moment. She held both her mates deep in her body and never before had she felt more connected to them. Oh sure, physically there was probably no closer connection the three of them could build, but it was more than that. The bond within them seemed to swell, and fill with a warmth and heat she had never experienced before, and she felt what they were feeling at the same time her own emotions and pleasure were building to epic proportions within her.

Just when she thought it couldn't get any better, it did. Both her mates began to move within her, in a syncopated rhythm that had her crying out as sparks of pleasure began to burst within her. She wanted to move, to be an active participant, but they held her still in their strong grips, and she groaned at how wonderful it felt to be held still and made to feel each and every thrust.

Soon, Violet was sobbing uncontrollably as the pleasure continued to swell within her. From the growls and curses coming from her mates she knew they, too, were fast approaching the tipping point that would drive all three of them into ecstasy. Jacob and Mason's movements became jerky, their earlier syncopation lost beneath the onslaught of pleasure.

Violet's release slammed over her unexpectedly, and she shattered. Everything within her seemed to just break into a million pieces, and she trusted her men would catch her and help put her back together again. She heard them both roar her name into the room, and she threw her head back and screamed.

When her awareness returned she was lying across Mason's chest, her heart still beating rapidly and her breathing rate faster than normal. She sighed and snuggled into Mason a little tighter and murmured in happiness when she felt Jacob climb onto the bed behind her, and pressed in close.

"Welcome back, little one," Mason's voice rumbled through his chest.

She lifted her head refusing to acknowledge that it took more effort than it should have. "Hey." Her voice was raspy, and she had a pretty good idea why.

"The bath is ready and waiting for whenever you're ready," Jacob said behind her, and she nodded, still not quite ready to move. The three of them then lay quietly together, and Violet had no doubt that they were all enjoying the simple pleasure of just being together.

Jacob sighed, his warm chest rising and falling at her back. "Mason and I have been thinking about IEH, baby."

Violet stretched between her men, feeling completely stated, but felt a flicker of fire spark within her when she felt their erections start to lift against her. "Oh, yeah? What about it?"

Mason leaned up to press kisses against her shoulder and she shivered when he bite down gently on the sensitive flesh. "Well, you told us once that you called it that because it stood for *Iustitia et Hyacinthinum.*"

Violet nodded, turning so she could look onto both their faces. "Justice for Violet. But as I said, no one knows that's what it stands for."

Jacob nodded. "But what if, just for us, we

changed the meaning to *In perpetua et Hyacinthinum.* Yeah, I know there's an extra word, but we'll call it a silent P."

Violet frowned as she desperately thought back to her lessons of old to remember the translation, and when it came, she smiled. "Forever for Violet. Well, I guess we could. I'm no longer all about the vengeance and the justice anymore. Santiago is dead, Chicago is safe for now, and I am with the two of you. So yeah, we could change it to that."

Mason grinned against her lips as he pressed a quick kiss to her mouth. "But it will have meaning for us, little one. Jacob and I, we are forever for you, just as you are forever for us. Marry us, little one. Be ours in truth, in love, and in marriage, forever."

Violet ignored the tears gathering in her eyes as she smiled up her mates. For the first time in her life she felt her ability to find the right words abandon her. Her heart filled to overflowing, she nodded happily, laughing when both men hugged her at the same time, murmuring words of love and unadulterated joy slammed into her down their mating bond. This was how her future was going to be from now on. Surrounded by love.

And having it last forever sounded just about right to her.

****

Roberto Santiago Dead.

The heading was quite clear, but the article beneath it didn't go into too much detail, and from the way it was written, it was clear that the journalist wasn't exactly heartbroken by the fact that Santiago was dead. He closed the newspaper with a sigh and pulled out his phone.

"Rossi."

"You see today's headlines out of Chicago?"

137

"Sure did." Rossi sounded almost amused. "Looks like Santiago finally ran into the claws of that shifter pack you've been warning him about all these years. Always thought they'd get to him sooner or later. You just don't fuck with men who can shift into fuckin' lions!"

"You may have a point, but you are going to have to work out a way to remove them from the equation."

His statement was met with silence for a moment. "How do you expect me to do that?" The light humor that had been in Rossi's voice just moments before was gone.

"Just like it's done in the wild, find a bigger fucking lion. I want Chicago back under my control in six months. Santiago fucked up, and his past and one pissed off little girl took it from me, and I want it back. Make it happen."

"And if I can't?"

Apprehension and fear. God, he loved to hear that in a man's voice.

He remained silent, letting it drag out until he heard a reserved sigh over the phone line before he said calmly, "Six months."

He hung up and placed the phone on the table beside him and looked out over the Adriatic Sea. The blue waters were crystal clear and almost seemed to reflect the blue of the cloudless sky. Six months, and he would head back to Chicago. He could wait that long. His vendetta was almost twenty years old. Another six months wouldn't hurt. Then he would finally have the chance to get revenge on that bastard, Murphy.

The End

www.maiadylan.com

EVERNIGHT PUBLISHING ®

www.evernightpublishing.com

www.ingramcontent.com/pod-product-compliance
Lightning Source LLC
Chambersburg PA
CBHW022029170626
46808CB00003B/1110